BIDDING ON LOVE

A Second-Chance Billionaire Romance

CHARLI CALLOWAY

Copyright © 2024 by Charli Calloway

All rights reserved.

No part of this book may be reproduced or recorded in any form or by any electronic or mechanical means, including information storage and retrieval systems, without written permission from the publisher.

1

Olivia

What the actual *hell* am I doing here?

I look down toward my continuous glucose monitor, which sits flat against my hip between the folds of my dress. It's bailed me out a few times since I got it put in six months ago. Being a workaholic means I often *forget* to keep track of the self-care parts of life.

My palms are slick. My hands are shaking. My heart is running into my ribs at a rabbit's pace. Normally, I'd be desperately checking my sugar levels, but I know this has nothing to do with my pump, which is dead quiet. Nope, this is all nerves. For a moment, I think about using my sugar as an excuse to bail, but I've never been good at lying to my big brother, Dom, and he and his girlfriend Maya will be here any minute.

I need another glass of champagne. Pronto.

Oh my god, what am I doing? A blind date auction? Seriously? Since when is this societally acceptable?

My assistant (and best friend since I moved back to the city after college), Gia, has been shamelessly flirting with the cocktail waiter since we got here. Normally, I'd support it, but her current position of tits-out seductive staring means he's not restocking on flutes, and both of our glasses are empty. If she turned around, she'd notice I downed both hers and mine. But I doubt Gia will, because the waiter guy is her type to a T: rugged, tall, tan, curly head of wild hair.

Unfortunately, I'm also pretty sure he's gay and enjoying the conversation about her new balayage for different reasons than she might think. No straight man has eyebrows *that* nice.

I don't believe in god, but something divine must be intervening when his boss calls him back to the bar. Gia watches him walk away, staring at his ass like a frat boy at a sorority party, and when she finally turns back to me, I'm midway through shaking my head.

"Really?"

"If you can't score at a charity event, then you can't score," she says. "I gotta prove I'm still back in the game. You know, since…"

Right. After she found out Kaden (her boyfriend of a year) was sticking his dick in his girl best friend, she's sworn off assholes and become vigilant about red flags. Lately, she's been dipping her toes in the pool of casual dating. Gia is gorgeous and smart, but she tends to have bad taste. Not that I can judge, given my love life has been dead in the water since my teens. Now that I'm veering a *little* close to thirty for my own liking, it's less *yaaaassss independent queen* and more *old spinster*.

"Well, I think you're barking up the wrong tree with him," I say, "But the guy by the bar, the one in the suit, he's been checking you out."

"Really? Where?" She starts scanning the crowd.

We're in a massive ballroom at a five-star hotel. The venue is dimmed with mood lighting, which reminds me a little bit of the cheesecake factory, but I suspect it was meant to be 'romantic' for the occasion. White tablecloths with electric candle centerpieces adorn each section. Waiters carry hors-d'oeuvres and champagne flutes on their silver trays, snaking between the aisles and offering guests refreshments.

I snort. "Nine o'clock. But be subtle. Be cool."

"Cool," she echoes, her cheeks flushed. "Right."

"You could always bid on a date," I suggest.

"You and I both know I'm picky. What if he's ugly?" Gia pauses. "I mean, no offense to you."

"Don't worry, I've been thinking the same thing." I mean this could be the guy to break my dry spell. I'm a little more worried about the personality as opposed to the looks part, but she's got a point.

"Besides, I don't have the money to blow on a mystery bachelor."

"Want a bonus?"

She shakes her head. "I'm just fine with my job and my salary the way it is."

I want to escape this place and get something to eat with Gia instead of being here, but none of the reasons to leave in my mind outweigh the facts. And the fact is, I need a plus one, and my *love life's DOA*, as the *Friends* theme song reminds me during my binge-watching sessions.

I'm here because Dominic and Maya reminded me not-so-subtly that I need a date for the 30-under-30 Women in Technology banquet sponsored by *Forbes*. It's an insane honor to have received the Woman of the Year award in the first place, but the implicit pressure to bring a date, to prove that you can have the career and the arm candy at the same time, means I have to blow the dust and cobwebs off the tombstone of my inner romantic. Unfortunately, I haven't been on a date in god knows how long, and I couldn't come up with a reason to nix the invitation and stay home watching *The Great British Bake-Off* fast enough for Dom.

Maya's perfume envelopes me before her arms wrap around my neck. "Oh my God, Liv!"

Maya is one of the only people Dom allows to share his nickname for me. He used to be a womanizing, devil-may-care type before her, but the second he looked into her eyes, he was lost. In typical man fashion, he couldn't seem to figure out his feelings for her for a long time, but she's unlocked something in him, some hidden ability to smile and break that stoic, stony exterior.

She's in a classic black dress that complements her bronze skin and makes her glow, even under the dim auditorium lights. Her wavy, ebony hair falls effortlessly over her shoulders, and the gold bangles on her wrist clink together, calling attention to her matching white-gold hoops. Her red lipstick is smeared on the corner of her mouth, and judging by the fact they arrived fashionably late, I bet my brother is to blame for any makeup malfunctions.

Dom is suited up in his sharpest Valentino suit and sleek dress shoes I'm certain are brand new. His Rolex, one of many in his collection, peeks out of his sleeve.

"You're late, big brother," I reply.

"I'm a guest of honor," he says, glancing at his watch. "Party starts when I get here."

"I tried to leave on time," Maya stage-whispers, dramatically cupping her hand over her mouth and flashing her immaculate manicure. My nails are a mess from picking at them, which sucks, because we got ours done at the same time not twenty-four hours ago.

"I believe it," I say knowingly. "Well, you haven't missed anything. Just some mediocre champagne."

"The good stuff is in the back," Dom tells me conspiratorially. "For us donors, we get good liquor. The rest of you get to partake in the watered-down stuff. I can sneak you another flute."

I shake my head. "It's fine," I reply. "I think the champagne is all going to my head. I'm dizzy."

Dom's eyebrows furrow. "How's your sugar? I can have the staff make you something to…"

"Dom," I interject. "It's fine. I'm all good."

I've never been the kind of person who lets anything hold me back—Type 1 Diabetes included. I was diagnosed with it as a teenager, and honestly, it was like a lightbulb went off over my head. Suddenly, a lot of things made sense. Unfortunately, with the Scooby villain unmasked, I was introduced to the challenges of sugar monitoring, diet, and insulin medications. Ironically, I used to be afraid of needles. Now, I stab myself like a pro.

I've always been the sort of person who works a little *too* hard, and when I'm not careful, I wind up realizing I need to eat a little late in the game. With my diabetes, that's not exactly an option, especially the older I get. The body bounces back a lot easier when you're fifteen, but definitely not in your late twenties.

My big brother has always been there for me, but he's also always been the type to smother me a bit. With the people I have feelings for or any assholes who take jabs at me at work, he's ready to defend me. It's nice, but sometimes, it's stifling.

Maya has gotten him to take it down a notch. Well, kind of. Now she's filling his head with notions of finding my Mr. Right like this is the early 1800s and the head of the household is the one who arranges marriage matches. It's sweet, in its own way, but I prefer not to have my brother act like he needs to defend my honor at every turn. Especially when my honor isn't really being threatened.

"So there are a few suitable candidates I hear," Dom informs me. "I'm not allowed to disclose who I nominated and which matches I find favorable, but I have to say that number—"

Maya elbows him hard in the ribs. "Dominic!"

"Right, right," he says. "Well, I guess I'll have to trust your gut on this one."

"Why did I agree to this?"

"Because you loveeeee us," Maya sing-songs. "I'm going to grab a drink before it starts." She bends down, kissing Dom on his cheek. The tiniest blush floods his face, and it's such a shift from the imposing, Bruce Wayne type I've come to know. He's a shark at work, but he melts for her.

Gia mimes a vomiting motion from her seat. "Do you two need a room?"

"I own this building," Dom replies dryly. "If I want a room, I could have any of them."

Gia frowns. "Weird flex."

He looks over at me. "Did you really have to bring her?"

Gia's grin is a little too smug. "Aw, Dominic, are you getting tired of me?"

"Yes. It's a shame I can't fire you."

"So *that's* why you've been hellbent on recruiting me to manage the marketing department," she chirps back. "It all makes sense now."

Gia is practically family at this point. I don't know why she's so hellbent on keeping her job as an assistant and nothing more, but she maintains it's about work/life balance and free time. That doesn't mean Dom and I haven't tried to get her a cushy job more suited to her incredible mind and talent, but no dice. For someone who loves to chatter, she's Fort Knox about this stuff.

Just as Maya returns with a dirty martini and slides into the seat beside Dom's, the lights dim, announcing the start of the charity auction. If it were women being auctioned off, I might have something to say about poor taste and feminism, but it's a fun twist for a blind date auction to be centered around men—gives us ladies the power. I'm still not quite sure how the optics are working out or how we've evaded the controversial label, but I'm trying not to worry about it.

"Welcome to our first annual blind date charity auction!" Bennett Hayes, one of Dominic's fellow "Balboa Boys" from childhood—his group of friends that made a nickname for their elite club—is the emcee for the evening. Like the other three, he's also ridiculously rich and handsome in a Henry Cavill way: Clark Kent glasses, sky-blue eyes, dark hair, sharp jawline. He doesn't look it, but he's the biggest extrovert of them all, and his podcast guest appearances have gone viral on YouTube a hundred times over.

"Each of our eligible bachelors represents a charity of his choosing. Because this is a *blind* auction, we won't be disclosing the identities of these gentlemen until after the bidding is complete. I'll be presenting a few fun facts and the date of *his* choosing. Ladies, he'll be all yours for a date of your choice as well, and upon completion, all of the money from tonight's bidding *and* a matching donation from the gentlemen themselves will be provided to the charity of his choice."

So every guy here is rich. I mean, I know the Bay Area is full of people with enough buckets of money to wipe their asses with twenties (and I happen to be doing well for myself too), but it still surprises me when discussions of hefty donations are tossed around as casually as one might describe the weather or football or some other boring thing I couldn't care less about.

Dom nudges me, holding up four fingers and mouthing it.

I roll my eyes, raising my brows and nodding towards Maya as if to remind him of her sharp, powerful elbows.

Ben loosens his tie a bit, chuckling to himself. "But that's all the boring stuff. Let's get into the auction, shall we?"

The room explodes with applause.

"Our first bachelor is a thirty-year-old Wall Street broker recently transferred from Manhattan to San Francisco's Tenderloin. He enjoys hiking, photography, and spending time with his single mom!"

While some people might find that endearing, if there's anything I've learned, it's that Mama's boys are total weirdos, and it's unavoidably true across the board. A guy has to be good to his family, but being a little too good means a can of worms I'm sure as *shit* not going to open.

No matter how handsome they are, I know better than to take a guy at face value.

"His first date is dinner at a gorgeous Michelin-star restaurant near the Wharf, followed by a helicopter ride over the city and Muir Woods!" Ben sets his cue cards down and claps his hands together. "Bidding starts at a thousand. Can I get a thousand?"

They roll through bidders, eventually getting up to twenty thousand before some soccer mom type with Botox in her cheeks freezing her face into position finally wins. My guess is she's a recent divorcée, but hey, everyone needs a midlife crisis, and it's for a great cause.

He turns out to be a handsome, shorter guy with giant muscles that fill out the sleeves of his jacket enough to make soccer-mom salivate over him. He's not really my type, which doesn't inspire confidence in the rest of the auction. I decide that if no one gets my attention early on, I'll just head home, download Tinder, and hope for the best.

"Our next bachelor is a thirty-one-year-old venture capitalist! He loves snowboarding, volunteering at his local animal shelter, and when he's not shredding waves or sealing massive deals, he can be found perusing local art and donating to sponsor vet fees for senior animals."

Oh. Okay, so he's actually perfect. Got it.

Is this guy even real?

I mean, I know Ben and Dom, and they vet everything they sign off on thoroughly. My brother didn't become a billionaire dicking around, and I doubt Ben will let anyone get away with deception if he can help it. But this guy sounds too good to be true.

"His first date includes a doggie day out sponsoring a rescue to find a new home and a visit to the San Francisco planetarium. Bidding starts at—"

"A thousand!" someone across the room screams, holding up her placard.

"Two thousand," I say, raising mine.

Maya smirks at me. "I told you someone would catch your eye."

We start rattling off numbers, and since I've already started thinking about how excited I am to kick off my shoes and get back to my apartment with my cat, Benedict Bridgerton, I'm hell bent on taking the sweet animal lover to my tech event and getting to bail before time is up.

"Fifty thousand!" I finally yell. We're not even close, but that's the maximum amount I've put aside for this ridiculous charade, and I'm ready to get back to my evening of binge watching and wine before work tomorrow morning. I don't have time to stick around if I want to find my zen before it's back to the grind.

"Sold to the lady in blue!" Ben says. "My lady, allow me to introduce Alejandro Hernandez!"

Oh. Fuck. No.

You know when you're reaching the crest of a rollercoaster, right before the moment your stomach falls out of your ass? That's what I'm dealing with right now. That feeling of falling off the edge of the world. My heart races with recognition as Alex, the only guy I've ever loved, the one I gave my *everything* to, rounds the corner of the stage and stands under the lights.

He's even handsomer than he was at eighteen. I've seen photos over the years of him and the other Balboa Boys, but in real life, he's even more perfect. That chiseled jaw with perpetual five o'clock shadow. His eyes, amber and molten whiskey. His curls. Fuck, he looks so good it should be illegal, and all six foot three inches of him is doing something to me, sending heat through my whole body.

You know, given the fact that he's Maya's brother, you'd think it would be hard to avoid him, but I've done a great job up to this moment. Clearly, my luck has run out.

"Unfortunately, ladies, Alex here belongs to the young miss over there, but as his friend, I can say he's an absolute catch, and it's downright criminal he's been single all this time."

Alex chuckles, and as he looks out into the crowd, searching for me, I've already started making a beeline for the door as fast as my ridiculous high-heeled shoes will take me. They click across the floor, growing faster and faster as I push open the doors and run into the cool night air.

I never should've done this. I never should've agreed to this.

My entire life has been sorted into boxes, organized

carefully to ensure I never tip one over, fall into the trap of becoming a moon-eyed girl again whose world revolves around a guy content to pull the rug out from under me the second I get comfortable.

What the hell am I going to do?

Just when I think it can't get worse, it does.

"Livvy?"

2

Alex

I'm a dead man.

The moment I realize I'm standing a couple of feet from Olivia Sterling, I take note of her caramel brown hair, her stunning green eyes, and the once-familiar curves of her body. I know I better get a look in while I can, before she drowns me in the fountain out front and buries my body in the underbelly of the nearest skyscraper. Before I can stop myself, before I can remind myself of the fact that I am very much on her shit list for the rest of my life, her name slips out of my mouth.

"Livvy?"

Mistake number one: announcing the fact I'm near her. Mistake number two: using an exclusive nickname from when we were dating back in high school. The nickname implies familiarity, friendship even. But we aren't friends, and every time I've asked Dom about her since, I got a very strong feeling she wanted me far, far away from her.

Ironic, given the situation.

She turns around—how is she more beautiful *now?*—and I feel like I've been caught, like when my mom saw me sneaking Coca-Cola from the fridge in the middle of the night as a kid. I'm under her scrutinizing gaze. I mean, Olivia went to Yale, and I doubt in the (almost) eleven years that have flown by, she's lost her attention to detail, impeccable mind, and ability to make any man fall to his knees.

"Alejandro," she says briskly.

Alejandro. So that's how she's playing this. I've been Alex to everyone since I was a kid, and she's never called me anything but Alex until now. I know the move is calculated. Without saying anything more than my name, she's drawn her line in the sand.

Well played.

"I saw you ran out of the auditorium," I start, "Is your sugar level okay?"

She looks down almost self-consciously. "It's fine." *Why do you care?* hides behind her teeth. I know she has claws, and I can tell that, whether I meant to or not, I've touched a nerve.

"I'm surprised you had time in your schedule for this event," I say. I've never been good at small talk, but I've also never struggled this hard with a conversation. I'm not nervous. I'm great at what I do, and generally speaking, I don't have to work at being charming. Unfortunately, everything about Olivia's demeanor says she's not under the spell.

"Well, Dom asked. If I had known *you'd* be here, I wouldn't have bothered."

"All the guys are here," I reply.

She scoffs, but when she takes her next step, her high-heels catch on a crack in the sidewalk, and one of them snaps. Just as she's about to hit the ground, I catch her, steadying her before I can think twice about it.

My arms are around her waist. Her perfume is all I can

breathe. I take in the flush of her skin, the curve of her beautiful mouth, and the fact her green eyes have softened from angry to startled for all of a moment.

Olivia. My Livvy.

No, not mine. I have to remind myself before I get too comfortable, before old habits threaten to overtake all of my good sense. Once, we were best friends, and then more, and now...

Now she's kicking off her shoes and stalking away from me, running her hands down the fabric of her dress to smooth it out, as if she can wipe me away in a singular motion.

"Is your ankle okay?" I ask her, watching as she wobbles over to the fountain and massages her foot.

"It's fine," she says quickly. "This is why I wear *flats* to work."

She wore sneakers to every dance in high school. For whatever reason, it rushes to the forefront of my mind.

"I can replace your shoes," I offer. The second the words leave my mouth, she turns to stone. Clearly, I've made some grand faux pas, though I have no idea what it is.

"I can afford to fix my own shoes," she quips.

"I just felt bad for upsetting you—"

"Please," she interjects, "Stop talking." She sighs, closing her eyes and catching her breath. "Look, I'm just gonna call a car and go home. Forget the shoes. Forget this —" She waves her hand at the building behind us. "*Circus*."

"And what about the date?" I ask.

"What about the date?" she says hotly. "I made a mistake."

"At least it's for a good cause?"

She shakes her head. "This whole night was a terrible idea. I should be at home. I have reports to write and a speech to prepare and a TED talk to coordinate. I really don't need to be here, in these ridiculous shoes, having a conversation with Satan."

I bite back a laugh. Satan? Really? If the tension wasn't so thick, I'd let the chuckle out. Instead, I bite down on the inside of my cheek to keep from smiling.

"A TED talk?" I ask.

"I got invited to do one. Or whatever. It's no big deal."

No big deal? I know her vision boards have always included opportunities like this, and even if I haven't spoken to her in a while, I doubt that's changed. I'm surprised she's downplaying it instead of rubbing it in my face. Maybe she's just trying to bore me out of this conversation.

"That's awesome. Really, Li—Olivia."

"You should go back in," she says. "I'm sure Dom would like to say hi."

I've spoken to Dom already, but I get the message. She doesn't want me to stick around any longer, and I'm not a pushy asshole. Besides, this conversation has only confirmed what I already suspected—she wants nothing to do with me, and that's never going to change.

"I'll see you later," I tell her. "It was nice talking to you."

She smiles stiffly, her mouth a flat line. "Yeah, you too."

At least she didn't call me Alejandro again. Only my *abuela* does that, and usually it's when I'm in trouble. Being a stranger to someone who was once my everything is a brutal thing to stomach, and to make matters worse, I have to waltz back inside, put on a show-stopping smile, and do some more networking.

The grind never stops.

My Thursday mornings are all the same: five o'clock wake up time, working out for a couple of hours, breakfast, take Abuela some coffee and drive Abuelo to work—if it were up to me, I would pay him good money to retire, but his pride would never allow it—and then I make some international business calls while I sit bumper-to-bumper on the Bay Bridge commuting to the office. I live in the city, but my family is about thirty minutes south in the small coastal town my best friends and I all grew up in: Sunset Hills.

Sunset Hills also features Balboa Hill, where the guys and I would escape to hike and ride our bikes down the steep, rocky slope. It's a miracle none of us cracked our heads open in the process, but for Ben and Miles, who always had it rough, it gave us a place to get away from everything. Hence why we started calling ourselves the Balboa boys. It's a cheesy relic from our childhood, but somehow, it's stuck.

I'll admit, when Dom asked me to join the Board of Investors for Sterling Innovations, I was skeptical. Most of my work is in architecture and humanitarian efforts, but after Dom fired one of the investors for being a Grade-A asshole, there were shoes that needed filling. He runs a successful company, and between him and Olivia, Sterling has become a tech powerhouse. I wanted to invest when they were nothing but a start-up, but out of respect for Olivia, I held back.

Time does not heal all wounds, unfortunately. It's a little late now to back out now, and I would never sabotage Dom's work. The best I can do is attempt to make amends with Olivia so we can be in the same building without burning it down. She's the CFO, so proximity is inevitable.

Not to mention, she also bought herself two dates with me. Two. Dates.

Bidding on Love

I asked last night about any way around it, and if we don't complete the dates, none of the money goes to charity. I doubt the event coordinators were expecting to deal with two scorned ex-lovers about to come to metaphorical blows (by that, I mean Olivia smacking me) in front of a gaudy fountain. As they were so quick to remind me, I signed a contract with specific terms, and so did she when she got her ticket to the auction.

Obviously, that's something to talk about. If I can even get her to look at me longer than two seconds.

When I step into the elevator, worrying about what to say to her, fate intervenes. Just before the door closes, a familiar hand pushes them open, and Olivia slips inside in the nick of time. As she steadies herself, I notice she's wearing a boot cast and a Converse sneaker. It's such an odd combination, given the fact she's in a blazer and pencil skirt. Outside of her footwear, she looks just as imposing as her professional headshot.

When she notices me, she sighs and hits the button for the next floor. "I'll take the stairs."

"With a broken foot?" I scoff. "I'll walk."

"It's a sprain," she says. "Dom made me wear the aircast. I don't even need it."

Given her four-inch heel snapped and the subsequent popping sound her foot made, I would say she's downplaying the injury. Dom may be protective, but he's not an unreasonable guy. Olivia has never let anything slow her down, even when she probably should.

"Like I said," I grumble. "I'll walk."

"It's far," she points out.

So it was fine when you wanted to walk it with a bum leg? "It's only nineteen flights of stairs. Who's counting?" I'm definitely counting. A two-hour workout including leg day was plenty for me. I don't need to follow it up with intense cardio.

"Fine. We can split the damn elevator." She huffs out a breath, switching her briefcase, pink leather of all things, to her other arm and taking the weight off of her injured leg.

"Look, I'm sorry again for—"

"Alex," she interrupts. "I broke my shoe because I have no experience walking in them, not because I ran into you. You don't have to apologize. For the last time. I'm fine."

My mother was adamant about me being good to women, but the problem with that, as I'm coming to find, is that sometimes genuine concern is mistaken for chauvinist bullshit. Or in the case of an ex-girlfriend, a greater plot to humiliate her. I have no idea what to say to her, and while my instinct is to apologize, I have a feeling that would just be gasoline in the fire.

"There's also the matter of the date," I remind her. "The donation doesn't go through unless we follow through. We both signed the contract."

She's looking everywhere but at my face, completely uninterested in me. If what I say fazes her, she doesn't let on. As the ultramodern elevator whizzes up the skyscraper, we listen to the terrible muzak and pretend this isn't the most awkward moment known to man.

"So we'll go," she says. The elevator finally stops on our floor, and she hobbles away from me as fast as she can. "Problem fucking solved."

Wow. I've only heard her cuss a handful of times before this moment, but this older, hardened Olivia is full of surprises, and apparently, a sailor's vocabulary.

Olivia and Dom have offices overlooking the Golden Gate and the Bay. It's a view I've only ever gotten from the top of Twin Peaks, and it generously pours in through the massive floor to ceiling windows like a technicolor painting.

I watch as she walks into hers and slams the door shut behind her, and then I head to Dominic's.

His door is open, and while his desk is covered in a chaotic array of files and papers and three different computer monitors, he's as cool as a cucumber. I don't know how he lives like that honestly, but not everyone is as particular as I am. Or hell, even Olivia. For as long as I've known her, she was the order to Dom's chaos. We'd all have been lost without her as kids.

His Rolex peeks out of his sleeve as he offers his hand for a shake. "Alex! Good to see you, son of a bitch. And on time, no less."

"Are your investors normally late?"

He shrugs a shoulder. "Never to meetings, but office hours are generally optional. Besides, post-pandemic most of them prefer to work from home, and a few are out of state. It's interesting to have one of you here in person."

"Well, I'm here to do more than throw money your way."

"Fuck knows I need your help," he confides. "There are a few operational things I need to take care of, and I'm up to my elbows in complaints and payroll. All of the stuff I should be delegating elsewhere ends up on my desk because no one does half as good a job as Liv and I."

"Let me help, D," I say. "Where do we start?"

Before we can dive in, Olivia materializes in the doorway, following by her assistant. "Dom?"

"Yeah, Liv?"

The bond between Dominic and Olivia is something special. He's so tall and imposing, but for his sister, he softens. He's her protector, her guard. If this were a duel, he'd be her second. Maya and I are close, but those two have a telepathy that makes me envious.

"I'll be taking my two o'clock out of office," she tells him.

"What two o'clock?" he asks.

"The prospective investor," she says slowly. "For the spot on the board?"

Oh? She didn't question my presence in the elevator, and I thought I was the only new recruit. I thought she knew I was being brought onto the team, but I'm starting to realize that assumption was entirely off the mark.

"I told you the role was filled," he replies.

"When?"

"Sent an email."

Olivia's eyes shoot to Dom's assistant, who sheepishly winces.

"The role is filled," Dominic continues, "Alex is stepping in."

Fuck me. If looks could kill, I'd be buried right now. He couldn't have told her sooner? Warned her before this moment, when the office door is wide open and everyone is eavesdropping? The assistant and I exchange nervous looks, like we're intruding on a very private, explosive family moment.

I have half a mind to walk away and give them privacy, but I feel like that would make this worse.

"That's why *he's* here?" Her face is so red it almost dips into plum. "Dominic!"

"The decision has been made."

"Without *asking* me?" The octaves her voice reaches when angry are shrill and unmatched, piercing the air around us.

"I did ask you. You signed off on the portfolio he submitted."

"It didn't have a *name* on it."

Even though I've always been Switzerland in the infrequent Sterling versus Sterling battles, I've unwittingly sided with Dom just by being here. No matter how little I knew about the situation, she's already assigned me blame. I can see it all over her face.

"And now you see why," Dominic says. "Olivia."

"You're an ass," she snaps. "I'll be working from home today, fuck you very much. Gia can take the day off."

With that, the ice queen storms away, leaving a chill behind in her wake.

3

Olivia

I might kill my brother.

I've definitely thought about it a few times over the years, when he's really tested my patience, but at this point in time, as I'm storming out of the building in what can only be described as a comedic shamble, I'm about two seconds away from ensuring our parents' house becomes exclusively mine when they die.

I'd call my mom and complain, but she made it clear a long time ago that on all matters of sibling disputes, she's staying out of it. Most people feel that way when Dom and I are about to start World War Three; it's best to avoid being anywhere near the conflict. We don't fight often, but when we do, it's usually pretty intense.

Yes, I suppose I did sign off on Alex's portfolio. Objectively, he's brilliant, has a fantastic CV, established connections, and a million and one reasons why it makes sense for him to join Sterling Innovations. But, Dom choosing to keep it anonymous knowing how I feel about Alex was so deceptive and *wrong*. An excellent strategy on his part, but a dick move.

Bidding on Love

I know this is why working with family is typically considered a bad idea. Working with your complicated ex-boyfriend is an even worse call. But my hand has been forced, and I have no choice.

I know Dom fired the old investor because the asshole was collecting sexual harassment complaints from HR, and if there's anything Dom won't tolerate, it's piece of shit men trying piece of shit stunts and acting like money makes them untouchable. He got the president of his frat expelled from Berkeley in undergrad for sexual misconduct, so his track record is consistent, to say the least. I was hoping he'd find some fresh blood for the board, but this isn't what I meant.

Fucking Alex.

He's like a splinter under my skin, and no matter how many pieces I dig out, he's still there, reminding me every now and again that I can't shake him or our history. He's a permanent reminder of the consequences of getting too close to anyone; a part of my life I left behind for good reason.

And he's also my brother's best friend.

My phone starts ringing the moment I pull my car into the underground garage of my Haight-Ashbury apartment building. It's a stylish residence with all the San Francisco charm, but it features impeccable furnishings of ultra-modern luxury. It cost a pretty penny to renovate, but it's my oasis. My safe space.

Dominic is calling. I send it to voicemail.

He calls again. Voicemail.

Then, Maya calls. Voicemail.

I have my day scheduled out, so it's easy to sit down in my home office and dive straight into my tasks. I'm great with numbers, so losing myself in all things financial for Sterling is the perfect escape. I take my spreadsheets, lay out the math, and blast my music until I'm sufficiently distracted and in the zone.

Theoretically, I could work from home forever if I wanted to. I prefer coming into the office and building connections with my employees. Dominic and I conduct meetings together. We create a personal atmosphere, which certainly beats the cold, unfeeling vibes of sending emails back and forth and navigating Zoom meetings. I've never once considered becoming fully remote, but now that I know Alex is going to be around, working closely with Dom, I'd rather saw off my own foot than walk into work again.

And I'm also signed up for *two* dates with him. It's rom-com level irony.

I get a few hours of peace, outside of client calls and business-related interactions. Thankfully, Dom grants me a break to collect my thoughts. The notifications slow, and by the time I'm nearing the end of my day, I feel like I've run a marathon. Often, whenever I'm dealing with feelings I'd rather forget, I do my best work, throwing all of my energy into it.

It feels like swimming laps and finally coming up for air. As I log off for the day, sending my final memos out, I'm awash with relief.

When a call comes into my work phone from an unknown number, I answer it, a bit confused as to who would be contacting me outside of any scheduled meetings or established digital interactions. It takes me a second too long to realize it's probably Dom or Alex, and when my brother is waiting on the other line, I grit my teeth.

Well played.

"Buzz me in," Dominic says.

"What?"

"Buzz. Me. In."

I sigh, checking the security camera for the garage. Sure enough, my brother's Tesla is at the front gate, waiting for me to let him inside. I have half a mind to hang up and ignore him, but he holds up a bag from my favorite Thai restaurant as a peace offering, and that convinces me to hear him out.

He's at my front door soon enough, all stony and annoyed at me for dodging his calls all day. I think he underestimates my ability to win the quiet game. I'm a master at the silent treatment, and when I'm pissed off enough, I take no prisoners and wage psychological warfare. One time, I gave my entire family the silent treatment for a whole week. Granted, I was thirteen, and rife with teen angst, but still. I'm just as stubborn as an adult. It's what makes me great at my job.

"You left work early?" I ask.

"I'm the CEO," he replies, "I do what I please."

"And you brought lunch."

"Early dinner," he says. "It's four o'clock. Did you forget to take your lunch again, Livvy?"

My phone beeps, the app connected to my CGM reminding both of us that my sugar levels are dipping. That answers his question.

He strides over to the fridge and pours me a glass of orange juice before he dishes steaming food out of the take-out containers for both us. Panang curry is the ultimate white flag, and he knows it.

"Truce?" he says.

"Ceasefire," I reply. "I'm sorry for storming out like that, I just didn't know... I wasn't expecting him to be *there*."

"I'm sorry for that, Liv. Honest."

Given how I rehearsed this conversation throughout the course of my day, considering the different ways it could go until I had a tangled knot of emotions in my head, I would've expected to be able to stand my ground. To be a shark, to be a woman in tech, which is an overly penile-driven industry, you have to be able to shut the emotions off, to be precise.

And Alex is an exposed nerve. Alex is my blindspot. All of my rules and objectivity fly out the window, because everything in me, my body, my brain, my heart, responds to him in a visceral way.

I never told Dom everything, but Alex broke up with me on prom night. Right after taking my virginity. I was so devastated I avoided him for the rest of the school year and signed up for the summer session at Yale just to get as far away as humanly possible.

I knew Dom would beat the hell out of him if he knew, and I was certain Alex, for all of his flaws, was a good person. It's just that sometimes, good people do bad things. Or maybe good people cosmically screw up before their brains are fully developed. That didn't mean I wanted him anywhere near me ever again, just that I wasn't going to sabotage my brother's close-knit friendship with his beloved Balboa boys. The four of them had been inseparable for as long as I could remember, and I refused to insert myself into that. He hurt me, but I knew if Dom found out the truth, it would hurt him worse.

There was one thing I knew for certain though, coming out of that breakup: boys were trouble, dating was a distraction, and the best way to keep myself from being heartbroken was to swear off romance entirely. It worked for a long time.

Now? My plans are off-course. My compartmentalized life is crashing down around me. He's my kryptonite.

I start to drink my juice, relieved that I'm going to be appeasing my rumbling stomach.

As we dive into the food, I see Dom nervously adjusting his watch. He's not the best at apologies, especially when it comes to admitting his pride, but I can tell by the set of his eyebrows that he wants to make amends. I mean, why else would he be here?

"Thanks for the food," I say, when the silence is threatening to suffocate me. "I didn't realize my levels were so low."

"Whatever you're thinking, Liv, just spit it out. I can take it." He meets my eyes, mirroring my expression. "Besides, we called a ceasefire. This is neutral ground."

I don't like opening up about my feelings. I like being on my game, and trying to decipher legitimate business concerns, such as our budget for the next quarter or what area of medical technology we'd like at the forefront of our recent investments.

"Fine. I'm pissed that he's working at Sterling. Wasn't it enough hiring your girlfriend? I know she's a marketing genius, but do we really have to make it this much of a *family* business? Come on, Dom!"

I pinch the bridge of my nose, sighing. Damn the good food. It's harder to keep up the anger when I'm eating something delicious. I love Maya, I love the Hernandez family. We grew up together, and maybe, if you went back in time and told my younger self that this is what our life would look like, we'd have been excited. But that was before. That was then, and everything is a hell of a lot more complicated now.

"I know you two have a history, but he's the best man for the job," Dominic explains. "I thought about it a lot, Liv. I wouldn't have risked hurting you if I had another choice. I looked at hundreds of portfolios and no one matched his caliber. I'm sorry, but we need him."

"It's not that I can't handle myself, it's just that I was

hoping to find a candidate who didn't kill my belief in love. What were you thinking? He's your friend and my ex, and the whole thing is a *huge* conflict of interest!"

"Total honesty? We also need Alex's money."

I know we do. I know the numbers better than anyone, and I know firing Douchewad McGee from the Board of Investors caused a ripple of doubt through the rest of them. The tight-knit group of investors requires confidence to continue placing their bets on our horses, and firing one of their own, one who was particularly gracious in his financial support, means Sterling could be balanced precariously on the brink of ruin. One investor already left in solidarity with his dickhead friend—and there were rumors others might unless we brought on a bigger, more bloodthirsty recruit.

We needed power, skill, precision, and a fresh face. Alex meets all of those criteria and has enough friends in high places to attract some new recruits the longer he sticks around. With an attractive candidate entering the Board, we're far less likely to lose anymore investors, and most importantly, we can avoid layoffs, budget cuts, and a PR nightmare.

I did debate in high school and college. I know, better than anyone, how it feels to stare at the other side of an argument, the one you absolutely, never in a million years, want to side with, and know that you don't have another choice. I have two business degrees *summa cum laude* from an Ivy League. I know exactly what we need to recover from the loss, and it's the opposite of what I want.

"But Dom," I say, pleadingly. "Did it have to be him? What about one of your other friends?"

"Alex is the most qualified venture capitalist I know," he tells me. And I know he's right. I know all too well how right he is. He's rescued companies from ruin, expanded profit margins wherever he's gone, like Midas with a gold touch. Not to mention, he's also a brilliant writer.

"Look," Dom adds, "There's every chance in the world he'll move onto greener pastures within a couple of quarters. Right now, he's our best shot."

"Our only hope," I add, throwing in my best (worst) Princess Leia impression to ease the tension.

"Next time, let's have the polite conversation sooner, without the whole office being able to overhear it," he suggests. "I've had plenty of nosy staff asking questions all day. Frankly, it's been obnoxious."

"Sorry," I say with a wince.

"It's fine." He looks down at his phone, chuckling.

"Who texted?"

"Maya," he answers. "She wants to know if you stabbed me with a chopstick."

"To be determined."

"Look, do you want me to find somebody else?" Dom asks. "Because at the end of the day, you come first. Our family always comes first. I'm sure there's an acceptable option, or maybe an investor wants to bring his son onboard…"

"No," I say quickly. "No, it's alright. We need him."

If this were about more than just me and my silly little feelings, I might be able to make the selfish call and vote Alex off the island. I'm a CFO, and I didn't get to my position by holding grudges or making immature moves. This isn't high school, and acting like I'm still seventeen won't get us very far.

Dom doesn't seem convinced.

"Really," I insist. "I signed off on him. If we forget the unfortunate ex-boyfriend part, he's a truly solid option."

That finally seems to satisfy Dom. As my big brother, I know he only ever wants to protect me. I'm sure as pissed off as I was, he felt ten times worse. I hate fighting with him, so being on good terms again is a breath of fresh air.

"You should know Alex wanted me to apologize on his behalf," Dom begins, "He never intended to cause a disruption, and he only wants to help our company and expand his investment portfolio. That's all. If you two can put all of the personal crap to rest, all of us will sleep better."

"I'll do my best," I assure him.

"Liv…"

"I'm doing my best!" I say more firmly. "We can be colleagues. We can go on a few civil dates for charity or whatever, but he will never be my friend again, and you can make sure he remembers that. We work together. That's it. That's all it'll ever be."

"Okay," Dom replies. "Then it's settled. Will I see you at the office tomorrow?"

I nod stiffly.

"Good." He takes me into one of his signature bear hugs, and I'm overwhelmed with love for my brother for a minute. Even when he drives me nuts, he's always looking out for me, and the reminder sends a pang through my chest.

"We're meeting with the whole Board of Investors tomorrow, right?" I ask.

He nods. "You can tell Gia she can add bourbon to the coffee if you think that'll ease the tension."

I shoot him a dirty look, brandishing my middle finger.

"Love you, sis. I'll see you in the morning."

Once the front door shuts behind him and the leftover Thai food is pushed into my fridge, I sit down on the couch, turn on my terrible reality television, and ice my stupid sprained foot for what already feels like the millionth time.

The ache is a reminder of two things: first, the importance of comfortable footwear, fashion be damned, and second, the way Alex's rigid, muscular arms caught me when I tripped. I'm a woman with needs, and being dangerously close to an Adonis-level hottie inspires a regrettably primal instinct in me that I'd rather not dwell on. It was a gentlemanly, gallant sort of moment, and it never should've happened in the first place and will never, *ever* happen again.

Damn Alex Hernandez. Even when we're rivals, even when we *hate* each other, he's all I can think about.

4

Alex

The catchphrase of my earliest endeavors in my career was: this could've been an email. So many meetings are nothing but empty conversations over burned coffee and stale pastries from whatever bakery is closest to the secretary's desk.

The first board meeting I attend at Sterling Innovations shouldn't be that terrible. After all, Dominic is a busy man who doesn't make a habit of dicking around when he needs to accomplish a million things in twenty-four hours. His work ethic is what got him here, and I have immense respect for everything he's managed to build for himself.

Admittedly though, I don't have a lot of confidence in the rest of the Board of Investors. Imagine Capitol Hill with its fossilized senators, and you have something like it here at Sterling. A bunch of geriatric white guys with fat wallets and a little too much time on their hands. I know what they're thinking when they look at me: young and fit without the need for a viagra supply. Being Mexican doesn't help. I imagine being taken seriously will be an uphill battle, but it's one I'm ready to fight.

Bidding on Love

I know when Dom took over the company and resurrected it from the brink of death, a lot of the original investors stuck around. After he expanded the medical tech company and revamped it with his name as the new signature, the Sterling siblings ushered in a new era. Sterling prides itself in the diversity of its hires and the freshness of its ideas, so the Board of twelve is the only relic of days past. The five virtual investors joining internationally are a bit younger and come from all corners of the world, but I know they're in a similar spot as I am. Seniority (pun intended) is everything here.

Olivia arrives right on schedule with her iPad tucked against her blouse, her chestnut hair wound tightly behind her head. Her makeup is natural, and the bright red of her lipstick has an effortless class to it that sends a bolt of electricity straight down my spine. Even with her boot, she's poised with that dancer's posture, her eyes scanning the room as she sits down beside Dom at the head of the table.

I hadn't seen her in years. I got so used to the occasional Google search, tip-toeing around my best friend because I didn't deserve to be around her. Now, all of the emotions I buried flood me. Regret. Longing. A wish to talk to her how we used to—like the only two people in the world.

"Good morning," Dominic greets us, rising to his feet. "If you'd refer to your devices, our quarterly finances have been shared virtually with all of you. Gia has also compiled a slide deck presentation, if you'd prefer to direct your attention to the projection screen. For our virtual company, I'll be screen sharing with you."

He nods at Gia, who types a few commands into the Mac desktop stationed in the conference room. She begins to click through the slides as Dom speaks. The presentation itself is sharp, and even though I've known the details since I signed on, it's hard not to be impressed as I listen now.

I'm not only proud of Dom. I'm proud of her. In every slide, there's Livvy's magic touch. Evidence of her prowess.

"Along with the reports of our profit margins and spending, there's also the approved budget for the fiscal year and payroll data," he elaborates. "So far, we're underspending with an increase in our profit margin. As you can see, Alejandro Hernandez has joined the Board of Investors, and his expertise will lend itself beautifully to our teams and investment interests. I'm confident that he'll bring fresh ideas to the table and further Sterling's legacy of innovation."

The lack of enthusiasm for my introduction doesn't bother me much. I knew I was replacing an old friend to most of the men here, and I know I'm entering as a traitor of sorts. That's nothing new for me, but if I backed down from a fight, I'd have filed for bankruptcy years ago.

Dom passes the mic to Olivia, who rises to her feet addressing the Board. "Pleasure to see you, gentlemen. It's our projection that, given the right reallocation of funds and investments, we can see a 9% increase in profits by the end of this upcoming quarter. The expansion will be essential for maintaining our clientele and advancing into new research methods for sustainable and accessible life-saving technologies, so it's essential to consider every possibility moving forward in this endeavor. If you'd please—"

Olivia proceeds to dive headfirst into her presentation. The spreadsheet and data are well-researched and calculated, but as I begin to do the math in my head, examining both the budget, the quarter financials, and her new plan, I realize there's something missing. If her idea could be expanded, maybe re-evaluated, there might be more options.

"Any questions?" Olivia asks.

The other board members shake their heads. For most of the meeting, they've been silent, disinterested in anything that doesn't sound like dollar signs and cash register chimes. Maybe I'm overthinking it, but as Dom's words about strategy replay in my mind, I find myself thinking ahead, how to take it all to the next level.

"Well, if there are no questions..." Olivia starts.

I raise my stylus. "Have you considered, on slide four, expanding the investment by 10%. Utilizing your calculations—"

She cuts me off, shaking her head with a smile that doesn't reach her eyes. With her lip curled so tightly over her teeth, her voice growing higher, I know exactly what she's thinking. "I assure you, I have considered it, and I'm certain my proposal is the most effective use of resources."

I sigh. *Am I doing this? Ah, hell. I guess I should.* "I'd be happy to provide you with a firmer grasp of the numbers, but I believe you could—"

"Mr. Hernandez," Olivia interrupts, her tone cool. "If you have any thoughts, feel free to share them with my assistant after the meeting. Given you're the only voice of objection—"

"I'd like to see Mr. Hernandez's revision to the proposal," one of the guys to my left chimes in. He looks old enough to fart dust, but he must be important, because the rest of them bob their heads in affirmation.

Olivia's eyes meet mine, and the sharpness of the emerald in them makes me forget whatever I meant to say. It's a look that could kill, to say the least, and with the encouragement of the rest of the men, she's decided exactly how she's going to gut me before we even conclude the meeting.

"I meant no offense, Ms. Sterling, I'm only suggesting that we—"

She interjects, and while her face is polite, the razor sliding under her words is not. "As I've said, you can share your thoughts with Gia. After. The. Meeting."

"I suggest the two of you collaborate," Dominic says, checking his watch. "That's all the time we have for today. I'll be sending an email with links to all of the materials as soon as their proposal crosses my desk. Thank you all for your attendance."

The moment the rest of the board files out and the virtual members sign off, the three of us are left around the table. Olivia's clenching her jaw so tightly a muscle tics under her skin, and her neck tightens.

Gia stands in the doorway, and once she reads the expressions on our faces, she shuts the door behind her. As soon as the lock clicks, all bets are off. I can only hope the room is soundproof, given what explosion I'm sure is about to detonate.

"Well, that was a fairly successful introductory meeting," Dominic says. "I'd say we have some promising ideas for the proposal, do we not?"

"I think with a little preparation—" I start. I don't even get to finish my thought before Olivia whirls around, slamming her papers and tablet onto the table and balling her hands so tightly into fists she quivers ever so slightly.

"Why did you do that?" Olivia demands. "You didn't think it was enough to accost me in front of the auction? Now you have to humiliate me in front of our investors? What the hell, Alex?"

"Accost?" I scoff. "All I did was *breathe* in the same public space as you and you're acting like I ran over your dog. What the hell, Liv? You're acting like I was trying to sabotage you or something!"

Everything in her eyes tells me I've run headfirst into the point and somehow missed it. I feel like I'm trying to win a game I didn't know I was playing, and reading her mind might have been a skill I had once upon a time, but she's stone now, and unreachable to me.

She takes a moment to steady herself, the way she always did in debate before eviscerating an opponent. "I have to fight tooth and nail to get any of these antiques to listen to me half the time. It took a couple of months before they stopped calling me sweetheart and making grabs for my ass. You just waltz in here like you own the place and start questioning me like I'm some kind of stupid girl. You couldn't have sent a fucking email, Alex?"

"It wasn't on purpose. If I'd known..."

"Oh, shove it up your ass," she sneers. "If you can't fuck right off your high horse, they're going to be demanding to have me replaced with the first small dick with an MBA. I get that you're not a woman and you're too caught up with your performative feminism to notice your own gender biases, but this is a man's business and I am fighting to keep my seat at the table!"

I didn't know any of that. Olivia has always been the kind of woman who makes the room listen to her. I never clocked discomfort in front of the board or opposition she was fighting against.

"So what? No one can ever ask you questions or challenge your ideas? You get to be the absolute authority without any collaboration? It's a miracle the company hasn't tanked and lost every investor if that's the environment you're cultivating here, Olivia."

She inhales sharply. "I have a rapport! I have an *understanding* with them. You're entering as an outsider, and the simple fact of the matter is that you're supposed to listen. You're supposed to listen and learn and then, maybe, insert whatever two cents you have into the conversation after a few meetings. Instead, you barged right in and started mansplaining *math* to me like I didn't set the goddamn curve for upper-level Calculus every single exam."

Maybe I should've been more tactful. I'm sure there are a number of things I might've done differently, given half a chance to think it through. I may have made an ass of myself, but she's definitely overreacting. In my experience, notes to expand profit are welcomed, but then again, the CFO isn't usually my ex-girlfriend.

This is new territory, for sure. If she'd give me half a chance, maybe I could figure this out. I doubt she's open to listening, no matter how many times I apologize.

I open my mouth, but before I get anything out, Dom finally breaks his silence.

"That's enough!" Dominic barks. "The two of you are acting like children. Again. For the second day in a row, I'm left wondering what drama is going to wait for me on the other side of that door. I don't need my company sabotaged by bickering and childishness. I can replace *both* of you if you can't get your shit together."

It might be an empty threat, but there's every chance in the world it may not stay that way. He's right. We're both smart and accomplished, and removing the complicated personal history, we could be a powerhouse team.

"You have a week to get this proposal finished so we can stay on track with our deadlines," Dominic says. "Then *together*, you can present it. Take a long lunch and expense it. Strategize. Apologize. Do whatever the hell you have to. Get. It. Together. We're on the same side."

Olivia bites her lip, sighing. "Fine."

"Okay," I say.

And then we all walk out of the boardroom like nothing is wrong, but when Olivia shuts the door to her office just a bit too hard, I know it'll be a miracle if we get anything done over lunch.

What surprises me, however, is the look on her face. It's not anger, not raw fury, but... hurt. Betrayal. And then it vanishes when she pulls her mask back on and gets her things together for lunch. The whole exchange has me unsure what to expect. Where do we stand? What now?

What the hell is Dom thinking?

We wind up at this vegan eatery over by San Francisco City Hall. It's not too far from the office, and the menu features a lot of Olivia's favorites from what I remember. When we get our table on the patio, overlooking the bay on the horizon and the hilly streets buzzing with traffic and people, she orders a glass of rosé and avoids my eyes as she spreads the contents of her bag out in front of her.

"Look, Liv—"

"Dom calls me Liv," she snaps. "Only Dom."

"Maya does too."

"You're neither," she says. "Anything else, Alejandro?"

"Fuck, Olivia, would you stop?"

Her eyes snap towards me, and when she meets my gaze, studying my face, she falters for a moment. "You don't know what it's like for me. How the board assumed I got the job because I was Dom's sister, or the rest of the hiring committee wanted to fuck me." She winces in disgust, shaking her head. "Look, I know you have your own struggles, but even though you're not a *white* man, you're still one of them."

I pause, feeling the weight of her words sinking in. While I've been fortunate to not face the same challenges as Liv, being the only Mexican American in the room of most board meeting I've ever attended comes with its own set of hurdles. Sure, a few of the board members might not be white, but that doesn't mean they understand my experiences or treat me as an equal. I've had to fight to prove myself just like Liv has, albeit in different ways. And that doesn't make her struggles any less valid.

"I didn't know, Olivia. I really never meant to undermine your authority. I just started doing the math, and I remembered what Dom said, about wanting me to offer advice if I saw something that could be improved. It wasn't coming from a place of animosity. I would've said the same thing to a man."

She shakes her head. "It doesn't matter."

"It does matter. I never want to make you feel small. I never want to mess things up for you." I sigh. "Now that I know, I'll be better next time. You shouldn't have to put up with it."

"It took two years to get the board to stop laughing at me behind my back, to stop speculating when I'd start popping out babies and not taking my job seriously." She laughs despite herself, taking a long swig of her drink. "But it doesn't matter. I should have a thicker skin."

I've never cared much for that idea, that people need to just look away when they're mistreated. I've always liked that Livvy wore her heart on her sleeve. I'd rather see her as the girl that used to cry over roadkill than someone hardened to everything.

She looks away, her lip wobbling for all of a second before she reigns in her emotions. "Right. Well, that's enough angst for one lunch, don't you think?"

"Are we going to be civil now?" I ask.

She raises a brow. "That depends."

"On?"

"If I can find a way to curb being so hangry," she says with a laugh.

The waitress circles back to our table and takes our orders for lunch. She grabs a salad and half-sandwich, I order a pseudo-meat burger I'm sure won't taste particularly great. That part doesn't matter though, because we found neutral ground, and she finally seems a little more at ease.

I know all the stuff that happened between us is old news by now, but she has me wondering what damage I did when I was nothing more than a dumb kid. I doubt it's the right time, not when we've barely found common ground.

Our eyes hold one another for a moment, maybe a moment too long.

"Show me the numbers," she says at last. "We have a job to do, right? Let's do it. Show me the numbers."

"Yeah," I reply. "Well, I was thinking if we start here—"

As I dive into my calculations, watching the gears in her mind turn as she checks my math, drawing the conclusions before I've had the chance to verbalize them. I always liked playing chess with her for this reason, and together, even our rough outline is something special.

5

Olivia

I don't date.

If a man were to say that, people might laugh, call him a playboy, describe how liberated he is. Career-driven and ambitious. When I say that, people ask me why I'm wasting time with a job when I could find a rich husband, or worse: call me a slut for being unattached and enjoying being young and sexy.

I'm out of practice with this kind of thing. My dates usually consist of a couple of drinks maybe once or twice a year, heading home with someone, leaving a few hours later, and collapsing in bed to watch shitty reality television until the blue light from the TV lulls me to sleep. Personally? I like my life that way. I enjoy the low-stakes, the ease. I enjoy the fact I don't have to try too hard or engage in conversations that get too deep. My usual tricks won't work with Alex for a number of reasons, but the most pressing being that first, we've known each other since we were in diapers and second, we work together. There's no bullshit or pretending.

Worse, I kind of bared my soul to him over lunch the

other day. It's not the kind of thing I normally talk about, especially not in front of Dom, who would fire the entire Board and screw the company over in defense of me before thinking it through. On the one hand, it's nice that he cares so much about me, but on the other, I can fight my own battles, and I don't need to ruin both of our careers over the sort of thing I deal with on a daily basis.

My brother means well, but when it comes to this sort of thing, it's best for me to navigate it solo, handling it all according to the laundry list of decent strategies I came up with the minute I decided to make my way in a world designed for men. Things like yoga, counting, screaming into pillows, fantasizing about bitchslapping them.

The point is, I don't date. I don't do this kind of thing: choosing a perfect outfit and freaking out over what the right thing to eat is at the restaurant and if I should offer to split the bill and a million other cliché things that never would cross my mind under any other circumstances. But here I am.

It's for charity. I mean, what could be a more noble cause than *charity*? And helping rescue animals? I mean, it doesn't get more perfect than that. I'm the kind of woman who kneels down to pet every dog I run into, and even if I have some unsavory feelings about my ex-boyfriend, it'll be much harder to hate him with an adorable rescue dog sandwiched between us. It's a built-in buffer.

My phone buzzes midway through curling my unruly hair. Just my luck that I'm having a bad hair day at the moment.

Alex: The limo should be out front in half an hour.
Me: A limo?
Alex: Hey, the auction demanded I go all out. If I'd known I'd be picking you up, I would've chosen an armored truck to make sure you didn't dip out before the date was over.

Me: Ha.

I read all of the fine print front to back, over and over and over, prepping for this. I know the date has to be at least three hours, checking every box on the itinerary Alex submitted when signing up for it. I know I could lie, but Alex is too honest for his own good, so I doubt he'd let me weasel out of it. There's always the looming threat of the contract we signed too, but for the sake of my sanity, maybe I shouldn't dwell.

The same rules are true of the date I select, though I'm not sure I want it to be the Women in Tech ceremony. If I could find a back-up date, without having to travel out of town with Alex, I'd consider that a win.

The anxiety that beats through my chest at the thought reminds me, sharply, that I have to consider the 30-under-30 event a future Olivia issue, because I need to be as zen as possible for this date.

We may not be at odds anymore, but that doesn't make us friends. It definitely doesn't mean we're date compatible.

A limo? That might work for someone else, but all I see is a beast to clog up Bay Area roadways, drain way too much gasoline, and emit enough carbon to make my Mercedes hybrid null and void. I get that it's supposed to be this grand romantic gesture, but in my head, it just isn't landing as anything more than a waste of time.

Like this date, for instance.

I'm pretty sure if you looked up *waste of time* in a dictionary, this would be a competitive listing. A date with two people who loathe each other? Yeah, right. That's about as pleasant as a colonoscopy or a root canal.

I know Alex and I shouldn't be like this, not after all this time. We're literally on the same team, in both work and in this case. I mean, what sicko wouldn't advocate for animals? Given that Mrs. Hernandez is a veterinarian, it makes sense that Alex has kept his heart and love for animals this long. It's a perfect date. Activity wise, not person specific.

When I finally settle on my outfit: light-wash blue jeans, a single ballet flat to contrast my hideous boot, and a pink cardigan over a baby blue tank-top, I feel good. Pretty, if not beautiful. I like to dress down when I'm not at the office, and comfort is my top priority in pretty much everything. Thanks to the fiasco at the auction, I will be steering clear of terrible shoes for as long as I live.

The limo is out front exactly on time. When the driver opens the back door to reveal Alex holding a bouquet of pink tulips (my favorites), I fight the smile that twitches at the corners of my lips. Okay, so he's looking handsome in a cream button-down and dark wash jeans and his shirt may be rolled up to his elbows, revealing those muscular forearms, but he's off limits, and I don't want to entertain the possibility of being hurt again. No matter how good he looks.

Oh my god, what am I doing?

I climb into the limo, sliding across the buttery leather seats. He hands me the flowers, and I look down at my lap, the intensity of his eyes overwhelming me. Alex has always had this way of looking at you with a striking attentiveness.

I compose myself, the parchment paper around the bouquet crinkling in my hands. "Was this planned by the auction too?"

"No," he says, a dimple indenting his cheek. "This was all me."

"And to what do I owe the pleasure?"

"I never show up for a date empty handed."

This detail elicits a memory I'd rather not be thinking about. It's true. I dried flowers from every single bouquet he brought me when he took me out in high school. I burned them all the night we broke up, and before this moment, I hadn't given it much thought. Suddenly, I'm awash with some all too familiar notions of affection.

"You date a lot?"

He frowns. "Define *a lot.*"

"Uh, often? Regularly?"

He shakes his head. "The only reason I did the auction, at the recommendation of the rest of my friends, was because it's been a while for me. I'm busy at work, and the long hours make every girl I've ever spent time with hate me, so I've found it hard to maintain anything. Not that I don't want to, but…"

"Right," I say. "Yeah, I get it. Honestly, I haven't been able to find any leads in the romantic department lately either. It's why Dom roped me into that stupid auction in the first place."

"Two workaholics," he remarks, chuckling under his breath. "Why does that not surprise me?"

"Because we were workaholics in high school?" I guess. Between the two of us, we had pretty packed resumés and even longer schedules. It's probably why we found success when applying to college, but it also meant the grind culture started with us pretty young, and clearly, stuck around.

I would've thought I'd hit burnout by now, but I've found that I like being in constant competition with myself, always trying to do more and do better than the day before. It's deeply rewarding, fulfilling beyond words.

"So our love lives are both DOA?" I privately think about sitcoms all the time, and the words slip out before I can stop myself. For a second, I'm embarrassed.

He snorts. "Is this really a moment for a *Friends* reference?"

"Every moment is a moment for a *Friends* reference."

When Dom and I were younger, we always thought about our friend groups to be a lot like the ones at the core of *Friends*. It felt sitcom-y too, for a while anyway. The Balboa Boys could've filled plenty of airtime with their antics, and the girls that always hung around them, myself included, made solid side characters. I liked to think of life as a sitcom, where everything was bright and colorful and light at the end of the day. Maybe things aren't that simple anymore, but call a spade a spade: I'm a glass half full sort of person.

Or at least, I'm trying to be.

"I catch the reruns sometimes at the gym," he says, "Ashamed to say I've actually started to *like* it."

Alex was never a sitcom guy. The only time he'd put up with my TV habits was when we could sprawl out on the basement couch and make out with one on in the background. We were crazy about each other then, and I was also crazy about laugh tracks and theme songs. It worked out well.

"How unthinkable," I reply.

"Maybe you were onto something all those years ago," he says.

Alex watching sitcoms? Hell must've frozen over.

"Dom will be horrified to know you've joined the dark side." The boys were always trying to get me to switch to whatever football game was on. I suspected Ben was more okay with my selections, but the rest of them never let me have a moment of peace.

"Keep this between us, yeah?" Alex teases. "Gotta keep some of my cred."

He broke my heart. I have to remember that, because I'm starting to feel the Alex effect. Every girl feels the Alex effect: he's tall and handsome and muscular and successful and—*and* a million other qualities that, sure, might add to his appeal, but in reality, don't make up for all of the hurt he put me through.

Whenever I start to forget, the old feelings push to the forefront of my mind. I hate to be a cliché, but the stories about remembering your first time forever are true. It marks you forever, and my first experiences with intimacy are clouded with the *after*. All the magic disappears. All of the love I had for him becomes hate and longing.

"So tell me about this dog walking thing," I say, worried I'm letting myself forget why I'm here, what this really is.

This is not a real date, Olivia. Not a date. Think of it like a meeting.

Hell of a meeting, another voice in my mind adds.

"Well, there's a sponsored doggie-day-out program through the shelter that attempts to get at-risk animals or senior dogs into homes. You can take them out for several hours, and hopefully, you choose to adopt," he explains. "Personally, Tuck has been lonely, so I think it's about time he gets some company."

"Tuck?"

"My rescue," he says. "He's a pittie I adopted a couple of years back. I had another dog who crossed the rainbow bridge a few months ago, and I think it'll be good for him to have a friend. So, today we'll talk about finding another match, see how they socialize."

I glance around the limo. "Where's Tuck now?"

He smiles. "With Mom at the shelter. She works there pro-bono on the weekends to provide care to the rescues."

Could they be a more perfect family?

I play it cool, staying coy. "You were going to introduce some random woman to your mother on the first date?" I ask. I mean, I know my love life isn't exactly something to tell great stories about, but I'm pretty sure there's something seriously weird about skipping ahead to

Bidding on Love

"Meet the Parents" within a few minutes of knowing someone.

"If it was anyone else, I may not have mentioned the mother part right away," he replies. "I just figured it would be hard to pretend you don't know my mom. Plus, she's excited to see you, and I bet you'll absolutely adore Tuck."

Sheepish smile. Scratching the back of his neck. I'm in trouble. It's hard to hate Alex. It's hard to think about him, stew in anger, and guard myself when he's being... Alex. Why can't he be like Dom with a rough, angry exterior? Alex is too approachable, too gentle.

He's supposed to be an asshole! I mean who leaves someone right after taking her V-card? That's, like, the ultimate dick move. Granted, it was a long time ago, and maybe he's different...

God, Liv, making excuses for him? You're in trouble.

Why the hell is he so sweet with dogs? How can you hate a guy who loves dogs?

"So if I didn't already know her, I'd be meeting your mom for the first time?" I finally say. "That would scare just about any woman off."

He interjects, "She's not going to be on the *whole* date, just while we're introducing the dogs and walking them. I'm not insane."

Part of me wishes Mrs. Hernandez *would* stick around for the whole date. Alma practically raised me when my own mother was out of town for work. I've kept up with her over the years and spent time with her whenever possible, but avoiding Alex and trying to keep up with his family is even harder than it sounds.

It would be nice to have a buffer. The longer we're around each other and the more he continues to be wonderful, the more I have to remind myself to pull back and avoid letting him in. I miss him, and following that train of thought is opening a can of worms I'd like to stay far, far away from.

"And then you want to go to the planetarium?" I ask.

He nods. "A gourmet dinner under the stars awaits us. I pulled out all the stops, champagne and everything."

Was this all planned in advance? I remember our nights on the back porch with the telescope out, chasing eclipses and comets and whatever constellations we could identify. Our younger years were full of pivotal memories under the stars. Is it a coincidence?

There's no way he knew I'd be the one to bid. There's no way he was planning on me even *being* there. But it's a perfect date, down to every single small detail from the tulips to the stars.

"Do you ever get tired of being a hopeless romantic?" I ask, keeping my voice light.

"Absolutely not," he replies, his voice almost sing-songing. "I figure if this is my one date for this year, I should make it a damn good one."

And so far, it's shaping up to be one. I have far too much pride to admit it, but he's weaseling into the cracks of my armor. "Well, I almost feel bad," I finally say.

"Why?" he asks, brows furrowed.

"For stealing some girl's perfect date."

In other circumstances, he would've ended this night getting laid, charming some girl into a few more dates. Even as a workaholic, this kind of thing would win any heart. He's irresistibly likable, for all his faults and best moments.

His eyes are smoldering as they hold mine. "I'm not," he murmurs. "I'm glad it's you."

I'm glad it's you. Four words. Four nails in the coffin.

6

Alex

I'll admit it: when I planned this date, I planned it around Livvy.

She set the bar for every woman after her. I know it isn't fair to weigh anyone in comparison to my first love, but it's something I do without meaning to. At this point, it's second nature to be thinking about her. I've been in love with her since I was twelve years old; it's not the kind of thing you can shake.

I didn't think Livvy would be the one *going* on the date. Not in a million years. I didn't even know she'd be at the auction, but maybe it's a stroke of luck that she ended up being the one to be out with me. I've never been great at impressing strangers, and I've always worried that it's disappointing dating me when I barely have time for anything, let alone socializing. Honestly, the whole thing is a headache.

I could make a million excuses, but at the end of the day, being a perpetual bachelor is absolutely killing my mother's dreams of having grandkids to spoil, and it doesn't seem like Maya and Dom have a kid in their five year plan.

The shelter my mother works for is affiliated with the Humane Society, sandwiched between a burrito joint, a boutique that reeks of different types of incense, and a gentlemen's club on the corner. It's a very San Francisco neighborhood with a Peet's in eyeshot and a three-story bookstore down the block. The traffic is bustling, and the city clamors with sound as we walk into the front entrance.

"Alex!" Paulette, the secretary at the front desk and my favorite of the staff, lights up when she sees me. She's one of my mother's best friends, and the smile lines on her full face and streaks of gray in her hair are comforting reminders of home.

"Hi, Paulette," I say brightly. "Is my mom around?"

"In the back with Tuck," she says. "He and your rescue for the day, Lily, are playing outside. They seem to be getting along."

"Fantastic," I reply.

"And who is this beautiful girl?" Paulette asks, her gaze flitting to Olivia behind me. She peers over the rims of her colorful purple glasses, smiling. "I didn't know you had a special lady!"

"Oh, we're just friends—" I start, trying to avoid making Olivia uncomfortable.

"We work together," Livvy adds.

Paulette raises a brow, but doesn't add anything, thank God.

"I'm Olivia," Livvy says, offering her hand for a shake. "Nice to meet you."

"Paulette," she introduces herself. "Do you two work together?"

"Sort of," Olivia explains, "He just joined the Board of Investors at my family's company."

Paulette frowns. "You look a bit young to own a company."

Olivia laughs. I'm sure it's the sort of thing she hears all the time, because she doesn't seem fazed at all. Maybe it's because Both she and Dom are insanely accomplished at a young age, and I'm proud of how far we've all come. Maybe it's because Paulette means it with genuine awe, rather than throwing it out as a backhanded compliment.

"She's the CFO at Sterling Innovations," I interject. "She undersells it, but she's pretty incredible. She works with her brother, Dom."

"Maya's boyfriend?" Paulette asks. "He's quite handsome, isn't he? Seems to run in the family."

Olivia blushes. "I'll let him know you think so, ma'am."

Paulette laughs. "Oh, don't call me ma'am. Makes me feel old."

"My apologies," Olivia says.

I never realized how radiant Olivia's smile is. Or maybe I just forgot. The way she lights up, charming the entire room and basking us all in sunshine... it's intense. Indescribable. I'm just glad to see her smiling, especially after how many times she's glowered at me in the past week.

"You better get out there," Paulette finally says, unlocking the door that leads to the outdoor space for the dogs. "Your mother is so excited to tell you more about Lily."

"Thanks, Paulette," I reply.

"Anytime." She turns back to the desk, shuffling papers around and pretending not to be watching us as we walk down the hallway and out to the grass. "It was nice meeting you, dear!"

"She seems nice," Olivia remarks. "I didn't realize she'd met Dom."

"She's my mom's best friend. She, Maya, and Mom get their nails done every couple of weeks. I'm sure you could tag along if you wanted."

She looks down absently at her hands. "It *has* been a while."

If she were my girlfriend, I'd pay for every manicure. The thought crosses my mind before I can stop it, and my surprise strikes me like a bolt of lightning. Thinking of Olivia as a girlfriend… that's a dangerous road to waltz down.

My mom is waiting outside for us in her scrubs, beaming from ear to ear as the dogs bob against her legs, sniffing happily. The second Tuck sees me, he rushes over, jumping on his hind legs to say hello. He's the sweetest dog I've ever met, and even though he seems a little intimidating, he wouldn't hurt a fly. I'm serious: even when one sneaks into the house, he pays it no mind.

Lily is a smaller mix with a tawny coat and a smile that sends her tongue falling out of her snout. She's friendly too, because she's all over Olivia within seconds. Olivia doesn't seem to care that her muddy paws are streaking all over her clothes, because she kneels in the damp grass, petting her with equal fervor. We'll probably have to clean up before dinner, but she doesn't seem to care, and neither do I.

"Hi! Hello! Oh my goodness, you're so precious!"

Lily licks her face, messing up her makeup, and Olivia couldn't care less.

Does she register how perfect she is?

"Olivia!" My mother lights up the second she sees her. "How are you, sweet girl? It's been too long. Why have you been keeping her from me, *mijo*? I didn't know you two were talking!"

I'm pretty sure if my mom had any say, Olivia and I

would've gotten married years ago. Mom took Olivia's side in the break-up, even though she understood why I had to break things off.

"It's a new development," I say.

"We work together," Olivia adds. She stands up straight, hugging Mom with an easy smile.

"You're so beautiful and so grown up!" Mom exclaims.

"I found a gray hair the other night," Olivia says.

"It only gets worse," Mom replies. "You're as beautiful as ever, though. Alex didn't tell me you'd be around! It's so good to see you."

"It's good to see you too," says Olivia.

"This means we can start doing family dinners again, yeah?" Mom asks, glancing between us. "I was thinking about making tamales this week. I remember they were your favorite, Olivia."

My mother taught Olivia everything she knows about cooking. Maya was never as savvy with it, and I never had an interest in the same way. Livvy was always having dinner at our place, and usually, she helped cook it, too.

"That sounds wonderful," Olivia gushes. "I'll have to check my schedule, but I'd love that."

Mom rolls up her sleeve, sighing as she checks her watch. "I have to get back to my patients, but it was so lovely to see the two of you. Take care of her, Alejandro," Mom tells me, her eyes stern. "*Te amo mucho, mijo.*"

"Love you too, Mom," I say.

She pats Olivia on the shoulder before she walks back into the shelter, and I smile over at her, holding out a leash. "You ready to take them for a walk?"

"Of course," she replies.

The dogs hit it off great. I've never seen Tuck have this much chemistry with another dog, but he seems to light up around her, all smiles and adoration. It's all too easy to confirm the adoption. The conversation between Olivia and me seems to flow as we take the scenic route through the city.

We drop Lily and Tuck off at the shelter so we can have dinner alone before I bring them back to my place. Both of us take the chance to freshen up in the bathroom, and while I didn't bring a change of clothes, I do my best to get the dog hair and dirt off of me. Livvy is already waiting for me when I emerge from the bathroom.

When we lock eyes, Olivia is still smiling, but a little pale. Her hands have a familiar shake to them, and the second I notice she's looking a little woozy as she sits down, I act.

I pass her a Dr. Pepper and a bag of peanut M&Ms—her favorite "quick and dirty" remedy for when her sugar gets low. I used to carry an emergency stash everywhere we went together. Hell, I even had her inhaler, even though she hadn't needed it since we were kids. Her asthma was something she grew out of, but I always preferred to be careful.

"What's this?" she asks, confused by the snacks. "Aren't we having dinner soon?"

"It'll take an hour to get there and wait for the chef to cook it," I reply. "Your sugar is low now, isn't it?"

As if her monitor is a paid actor, her phone starts beeping. She blushes, tearing into the candy with a shy look. "I can't believe you remembered."

"I can't believe you have the same snacking habits as you did when we were seventeen," I reply.

She rolls her eyes. "If it ain't broke…"

"Why aren't you carrying anything?" I ask. "Did you sacrifice practicality for the cuter purse?"

Her Saint Laurent bag is adorable, but it's far too small and doesn't have nearly enough space in it for everything she needs to carry. If there's anything I know about Olivia, it's that she runs at a hundred miles an hour all the time, and sometimes, that means other things fall by the wayside, like her health.

"Call it poor planning," she says between bites. "Just give me a few minutes to sit."

"You really think I'd rush you? I'm pretty sure if you collapse from low sugar Dom will bury me, and that's *after* my mother kicks my ass. I'd never leave you high and dry."

"Well, not everyone is as patient as you are," she replies. "I had this friend in college who used to get pissed at me if my sugar dropped at an inconvenient time for her. She didn't drive, so I was her chauffeur, and my 'issues' impeding on her schedule always made for conflict."

"She sounds like a bitch," I remark. "Jesus, Livvy, I'm sorry."

I'm not sure what I'm expecting her to say or do, but she just pops a handful of chocolate into her mouth, chewing with furrowed brows as she sinks into her thoughts. She softens for a minute, her eyes holding mine.

"Why do you do that?" she asks. "Call me Livvy? We're not… You know we…"

"Force of habit," I say.

Livvy. She was always Livvy in my arms, and I feel like the sides of her I see, the way I know her, is far more personal than just calling her by her government name and calling it a day. I know that's a level of comfort we're not at anymore though, and it would be foolish to act like there aren't years of questions and animosity to move past. I'm not sure if it would do us any good to tell her the truth about why we broke up, why I broke both of our hearts. It feels like digging up the grave, insult to injury.

"I'm not your responsibility anymore, Alex," she reminds me. "I appreciate the gesture, I do, but you don't get to pretend nothing ever happened between us, and this date is for charity. We're better off if nothing is misconstrued."

I want to ask her what could possibly be misconstrued or what she even means by it. I don't think there's anything happening here beyond spending longer than a few minutes without tearing each other's heads off, but she's looking at me like this is some angle I've been working at and she wants me to know she's not falling for it.

As far as I know, the best move is to disengage. So I clear my throat, I catch my breath, and I smile stiffly at her.

"So dinner," I say.

"So dinner," she echoes.

As soon as her sugar is back to a decent level, we head into the limo. It's awkward, the ride, and the air around us feels thick, but I do my best to occupy myself with station surfing on the radio and avoiding prolonged eye contact, like I'm in a cage with a tiger or something.

Not that Olivia is a tiger, because I'm pretty sure she'd kill me if she knew I was even thinking that.

If I hadn't gone into business, I think I would've gotten into astrophysics or astronomy. Business felt like the more practical option, though admittedly, I wonder what my life would've looked like if I'd taken another path. The planetarium is a place I have a season pass to, and I go often when I need to escape or make everything feel a little more manageable. I'm often at the end of my rope and doing my best to tread water when the week is wrapped up and my fourteen hour days finally slow down. Being grounded under a sky far more infinite than me always puts it into perspective.

I pulled quite a few strings to get us here—made phone calls, paid a lot of money. It's all worth it for her, though. As we crack open a sparkling wine, which is aptly named *Andromeda* with some Italian label I can only partially read, she glances around us, taking in the vastness above us.

"I remember when we took a field trip here in third grade," she said. "They showed us the sky in the future, predicting the patterns of the stars and planets."

I also remember she got scared in the dark before the starlight turned on, and I took her hand as we laid down listening to the teacher shush all of the wild kids in our class. She was wearing a skirt with rainbow tulle, and when she glanced over at me in the dark, her eyes were so bright they could've been their own planets.

God, I'm so pathetic. I am haunted by memories.

"You think they got it right?" I ask her.

"Can't remember. I definitely didn't think I'd be here in my adult years though."

"What do you mean?"

She snorts. "Well, as far as I was concerned I was going to marry a European prince and be a princess of a small nation somewhere across the pond."

I remember she wore a tiara for career day when we were in school for a couple of years in a row. Dominic beat up any kid who made fun of her for it. She lived happily in her bubble until her dream was to take the presidency by storm because boys had cooties.

"And I was going to be an astronaut," I remark. "Too bad I'm terrified of blowing up like the Challenger." That library book was enough to traumatize me from the possibility. It took me a few tries to figure out what I really wanted to do at the end of the day, and I didn't wind up here until halfway through college when it clicked in my brain.

"Seems like we were both wrong," she says.

"Seems like it."

We're a far cry from the boy in a Giants jersey and the girl in the rainbow skirt, but there's something about this moment, having dinner under the stars, that doesn't feel so different from the past at all.

It is different. Of course it is. But in the dark, I can pretend.

7

Olivia

Alex is in my bed.

I feel the heat of his body against mine, his strong, solid arms encircling me around the waist. We're completely bare, and the sensation of his touch, awareness of all the places our bodies stick together, every nerve in me at attention for him, has me insane. I feel him lean in, pressing his mouth to the side of my neck and tracing kisses down the slope until he lands on my shoulder.

His voice is a sexy rumble against my skin. "Good morning."

"Morning," I whisper.

One of his palms slides lower against my stomach. "Think we have time for a quickie before work?"

"I—"

My alarm blaring startles me out of the dream. I shoot upward in bed, gasping for breath and clawing at my chest. My worn Yale t-shirt is damp with sweat, and my heart is hammering against my ribs. It's not with the adrenaline of a nightmare, though. No, this is worse. This is pure arousal.

I just had a dirty dream about *ALEX*.

I mean, I guess it wasn't the first time it's happened to me, but when you're in a relationship, sex dreams are fine. What's not fine is having them about your pseudo-enemy that you're forced to be in a collaborative relationship with. That definitely crosses into dangerous territory. Things I don't want to touch with a ten-foot pole territory.

I fall out of bed and into the shower, hoping to scrub away the reminders of the NSFW thoughts I was having about him just moments before. More than anything, I'm embarrassed.

The date yesterday was a little too great: him clocking my sugar just seconds before my monitor, time with his adorable rescue dogs, seeing Alma for the first time in years, and a fantastic dinner in one of my favorite childhood places. Everything was great, and if it was with a total stranger, it's the kind of date that would end with a nightcap and sex.

Apparently, my subconscious mind thought so too. It's an uncomfortable revelation, and it's definitely not a welcome one. Knowing Alex is attractive is different than being reminded of how attractive I find him, and my brain seems to have decided I have no choice in the matter.

Alex Hernandez is completely off-limits. He's not allowed to be more than a passing thought, because I know what happens when I don't guard my heart. The second I get comfortable, the rug gets pulled. We were best friends who finished each other's sentences. I was known, completely and utterly, by him. It was everything.

I was in love once. One time is plenty for me. I have a job to focus on, and worrying about finding a boyfriend feels as unimportant as picking out the perfect outfit for a high school dance. It's not something I need to concern myself with.

Alex and I finalized our proposal, and today we present it again to the Board of Investors. This meeting is primarily virtual, but Dom, Alex, and I will all be in-office. The barrier that Zoom provides doesn't make it any easier to swallow my pride and deal with the fact the last board meeting went poorly for me, and now I'm under the skepticism of a few prehistoric relics with fat wallets and internalized misogyny.

As I'm washing and drying my hair, careful not to put weight on my bad leg while I'm not wearing the boot, I'm thinking about the fact that these problems probably wouldn't be my burden if I was a guy, but that's sort of the luck of the draw. At this point, I'm used to it.

The air cast gets to come off next week, thanks to the fact my sprain was on the milder side. I probably would have lived without the cast, to begin with, but Dom riding my ass would just be another problem I don't have time for.

The walk on Saturday was super easy, and honestly Alex didn't let me take many steps at all, but I still feel a little sore. The reminder of how I spent my weekend on a date with someone I have a terribly complicated history with is just the cherry on top of a crap sundae. Especially given the raunchy nature of my dreams, it's not a great time to be carrying around unshakeable reminders of my pesky subconscious feelings for him.

Why does he have to be so likable? I want to hate him. I'm supposed to hate him. I'm supposed to be fantasizing about kicking him in his stupid face for what he did to me, but it turns out, holding a grudge is harder after an extended period of time, a lot of growing up, and lots of good memories to replace the old, terrible ones. Hindsight is obnoxious, and while I *thought* my brain and I were on the same page, I've come to find that my dreams missed the memo.

One more date. I have one more date with Alex, and then we can go back to being ships in the night who happen to work together and occasionally bump into each other at the coffee pot in the shared kitchen. That division is a good thing to maintain in the long run, especially because adding complexity at a time of my life where I don't have the emotional or mental space for it isn't ideal.

The budget proposal with Alex's modifications is strong, I'll admit. He definitely has an eye for numbers and incorporating outside-of-the-box strategies I hadn't considered. Because his business background is so varied, he's found plenty of means to optimize our financial resources that promise to drive our company's growth forward.

He let my original work provide the base for our changes, and at the end of the day, deferred to my judgment so as not to step on my toes. It was the most gentlemanly work collaboration we could've possibly had, and I'm not sure how I feel about it. Grateful sure, but something else I can't place, too.

I get dressed for work, pick my favorite white gold hoops out of my jewelry box for luck, and head downstairs after dropping a few pats on Benedict's furry little head. The nice thing about having a cat is he seems to be generally indifferent to me and allows me to have a busy work schedule in peace, but admittedly, he's never all that excited for me to come home after a long day. Maybe that's why Alex has dogs—there's always someone to keep him company and love him unconditionally.

Thankfully, there are no surprise ambushes in the elevator on the way up to the office. As the lift climbs dozens of floors, I lean onto my good leg and run the script of my proposal over in my mind. I plan every presentation down to the second, when to take breaths, when to switch slides, when to drop numbers and open the floor to ask questions. Dom has always been the kind of speaker who improvises and charms the room, but I prefer to plan.

Alex is waiting for me in the conference room with two cups of coffee. When he passes me a whole milk latte, I pause, tracing the label. "You remembered?"

"It's more like a took a gamble," he says. "I didn't know if it changed in the last ten years."

"A lot of things did, but good coffee? Nope. I know what I like."

"Decisive as ever," he remarks.

"Right."

He glances down at his tablet, tucked against the sleeve of his charcoal Valentino suit. "I proofread the figures on the treadmill this morning. Everything is golden; you take the lead, and I'll follow."

"Thanks."

I can tell by the way he licks his bottom lip, tucking it between his teeth, that he wants to say something and doesn't know quite how to get it out. It's the same look he wore when we were kids, and he nervously fumbled his way through asking me to be his girlfriend. Weighted. Calculated. Unsure of what to say, but knowing he's dancing around it.

Before he can get it out, Dom walks into the room, and he and Gia get to work in setting up the Zoom conference onto the projection screen on the wall across from the table. As the investors log into the meeting one by one, I swallow my beating heart, and we begin.

Alex is just as good as Dom at these things. He has a melodic voice that presents secondarily to me, but I'm feeling self-conscious, even if I know I don't have to prove anything to anyone. The fossil types are usually pretty floored by a *woman* CFO. The fact the rapport is fragile enough to get knocked down by a new guy entering the picture is annoying, but I'm used to it.

When it comes time for the question section of the meeting, the first guy to speak up peers skeptically over the lenses of his thick glasses, and even though I can't be sure, I'm pretty certain he's staring at me.

The question he asks is relatively simple, and it's one I'm pretty sure I covered in my initial presentation last week. I have half a mind to thank the universe for the softball question, but as I open my mouth to answer, he barely lets me get a word out.

"If Mr. Hernandez was the one proposing these changes, why are *you* answering my questions?" he asks. "Seems odd that you would speaking for him."

Alex shakes his head. "The changes made to the proposal were all based on Ms. Sterling's calculations, data, and thoughts. I merely asked a few questions. The brunt of the work is hers, and she continues to work tirelessly at perfecting our budget and strategies. Admittedly, I don't know jack shit about this stuff the way she does."

I open my mouth to say something, to continue my train of thought and stand up for myself, but despite the pissing contest being about *me*, it doesn't seem as though anyone cares what I have to say on the subject.

"I think you afford her far too much credit," the board member says.

Dominic cuts in, "I don't appreciate your tone—"

Alex's expression hardens, and his low voice cuts through the room. "I assure you, I have more money than I need. Trust me when I say I can match your contributions and probably double it. So if you have no respect for what Ms. Sterling is doing here, what all of us are doing here, you can fuck right off," Alex says. His voice is low, cold. It strikes me with a chill down my spine. "Understood?"

This testosterone-filled mess isn't going anywhere productive, and I may not be a psychic, but I'm certain I don't have to be able to see the future to know this needs to end before things escalate. So, I throw on my most patient smile and clap my hands together.

"I think we can call it here," I say. "Thank you all for your time. Feel free to contact me with any additional questions."

As they log off, I collect myself, finishing the last of my coffee like it's a shot of liquid courage. Normally, I appreciate how much Dom cares, how much he'll fight for me, but right now, I wish he'd back off a bit. Lately, he's been suffocating me.

And now Alex too? Honestly, who do they think I am?

Dom starts, "Liv—"

Alex says, "Look, I—"

"What the hell?" I demand. "I don't need either of you to defend my honor, and especially not you, *Alex*. One backhanded comment isn't anything to get upset about, and I'd rather not lose any investors or let them continue to think I need to be replaced. Stop. Talking. Over. Me."

He takes a second, working it over in his mind, chewing on his lower lip. A muscle tics in his jaw, and finally, after what feels like an agonizing eternity, he nods. The apology swirls in the whiskey of his eyes, even if he doesn't say it aloud.

I turn to my brother next, shaking my head. "And you, Dom? You need to calm down, because if you keep firing investors the second they piss you off or show their misogynistic colors, we'll go under before the year is up. That can't happen, and you and I both know there's a lot riding on what Sterling Innovations does. Get. It. Together."

God, my head hurts. I told Dom it would get messy working with too many family and friends, but he didn't listen, and now I'm continuing to see the proof of that play out right in front of my face.

I continue speaking, my jaw clenched. "I have fought my own battles for years. I don't need you to do it for me, and it's humiliating to hide between you two, whether it's intentional or not. I earned my way here, graduated *summa cum laude* from Yale. I can handle this."

I can handle this. It's something I've told myself and sworn up and down for as long as I can remember. I don't know what it is about reminding the two of them of that fact, but it hits me hard in the chest. I never wanted to prove anything to them, and until just now, I didn't think I ever had to.

I steel myself, blinking the tears of frustration away. "I need a moment alone. I'll be in my office."

I shut the door behind me, but unfortunately, the damn doors don't lock. I don't know why we didn't put locks in during the remodel, but it would come in handy right about now. It sucks when I want privacy. No, when I *need* privacy.

When someone knocks not five minutes after I've sat back down at my desk and remembered how to breathe, it takes everything me not to snap like a paper thin rubber band.

"What part of needing to be alone do you not get—"
"I'm sorry."
Maya standing in my office surprises me. "I know you had a rough meeting, and I figured it was probably a lot

better for me to be here as opposed to my brother or yours. They're the worst sometimes, aren't they?"

"You have no idea."

"I think I do," she says lightly. "Your brother sleeps at my place half the time. It's never been messier."

"He's basically helpless," I reply with a snort. "I don't know how he manages a corporation like this, but he's an absolute slob. It drives me nuts. Up the wall, in fact."

"And now he's my responsibility."

I've never seen two people more in love than Dom and Maya, though. The two of them challenge each other like hell, and whenever they're together, they bring out a light in each other I've never seen before. It's a happy responsibility. It's all over her face.

I groan, and the exasperated sound is almost a screech as it tears from my mouth. "And your damn brother is always pushing himself into my business! Who does he think he is, Maya?"

I can think of a million answers to my question.

"He must be a glutton for punishment," Maya says. She pauses, taking a second to think. "Look, does Dom know what happened between you two? Does Alex?"

"It's old news. We've managed to figure this out. We can be civil."

"I don't think Alex knows how to be civil with you. He jumped in to defend you because he can't imagine not having you in his life. He doesn't want to be strangers anymore." She takes a second, thinking it through before cutting herself off. "Well, I'm not going to speak for him, but he definitely wants to be your friend. And he's probably gonna make an ass of himself until he feels like he's making progress."

"Then why did it take him so long to get here?" I ask. "If he wanted to be friends."

"Would you have given him half a chance?"
The answer is a resounding no.
"Thank you, Maya."
She shrugs. "For what?"
"Being here."

8

Alex

After the day I've had, drinks with the rest of the Balboa boys is exactly what I need. We have a spot not too far from Twin Peaks, which sits right in the center of San Francisco. It's exactly between all of our apartments, and even though it's not as high profile as the places we frequent for work, it has the dive bar feel of the places we'd sneak into when we were underage.

Bennett, with his thick Clark Kent glasses, is here first. He's chronically early, always has been. I never know how it doesn't drive him nuts, but somehow, it's tried and true for him. He's changed out of his business clothes and switched to a flannel and worn blue jeans, which is ironic, given Miles is the one in construction.

After Dom and I trickle in, Miles arrives last. His tie is loose, and a few of his buttons are messily done. With his black hair mussed, he's all trouble. His Italian genes and naturally tanned skin make him a serious womanizer. He always has a date. And it seems like tonight, when he's half an hour late, he had a date that ran long.

"Another quickie, Miles?" Ben asks, crinkling his nose.

"You know Mondays are beer nights. And fantasy football catchup."

"Valerie is smokin hot. If you saw her, you'd know exactly what I mean." He makes a *perfect* sign with his fingers for emphasis, pushing a hand through his hair. He's covered head to toe in tattoos, and I can see a few of them dark through his white shirt.

"I've been there," I say. "Sometimes, a girl just hooks you. Makes you lose track of everything." The second the words leave my mouth, I wince. Hopefully no one asks me to disclose *who* is on my mind.

"Maya can't keep her hands to herself sometimes," Dom chimes in. "Makes us late to everything."

Ben rolls his eyes and scoffs. "So *that's* why you rolled into the auction at the last second."

"I was a big fan of her dress," he says with a wink.

"Dude, that's my sister you're talking about," I groan. "Can you imagine if I made comments like that about Olivia?"

I've always been private, semi-allergic to PDA. Maya and Dom are the opposite. It's nice to see her happy, but I can't fight the brotherly urge to gag when he talks about how sexy she is.

Dom scoffs. "Consider us even for all the times you sprung a boner when Liv walked into the room in high school. That was nasty."

Right. I hate when he talks about my awkward phase. There's something kind of beautiful about the way friendships, the kind that span years, mean seeing every version of each other and watching each other grow up. Unfortunately though, it also means we have memories of pimples, unrequited boners, and brutal teenage years.

"So what's new with you, Alex?" Ben asks. "You and

Dom couldn't get enough of each other and needed to take the bromance to work."

Dom jokingly takes my hand. "You're just jealous you can't join us."

I take my hand away. "You're unreal, man."

"This unresolved romantic tension kills me," he says with mock offense.

"You trying to collect the Hernandez siblings?" Miles jokes. "Need the full set?"

I chuckle. The four of us are always able to laugh together, and the number of inside jokes we've accumulated always makes me nostalgic. Never gets old. I always worried we'd get tired of each other the older we got, but it doesn't seem like that'll slow down anytime soon.

As Dom and Ben head to the bar to get another pitcher of 805 pale ale, Miles seizes the moment to get a little TMI with me. I know the stereotype is that guys don't gossip, but Miles especially has plenty of *chismé*, as my mother would put it.

"So how is it being hot for the boss, Alex?" Miles asks, winking at me.

"Is everything a porno with you?"

"Could be. I have a creative vision."

I scoff. "Right. That's what they're calling it now."

Miles plays the goofy playboy, but he's wicked smart and a brilliant architect turned construction guru. It's impressive what he's turned a hobby into, and he works insanely hard. Beneath the tattooed exterior, I know he also has a good heart, but after the girl he wanted to marry died a couple of years back, he's sworn off love and resorted to drowning his sorrows in… Well, I'm sure you can guess.

The last thing I want is to talk about Olivia. She's my ultimate weak spot. Thinking about her is a slippery slope into what ifs and past mistakes. That would eat anyone alive, and I often find myself consumed with thinking about her. Every step we take, I'm reminded of how many things I've done wrong, how much I wish I'd done differently.

Not to mention, I'm a single bachelor, and she's a beautiful woman. That part is just nature, and it complicates *literally everything else*. Miles is looking for a reaction, though, and I'm not gonna give him one. I don't need him to hound me for the next week until he gets bored.

"She's not my boss." I pause. "Well, actually I'm not entirely sure what she is. Point is, it's not like that. Believe me. I think she'd kill me if she even *thought* I was getting the wrong impression."

"Sounds like Olivia," says Miles. "She's a pistol, isn't she?"

"Watch it," Dom warns. "That's my sister."

"Should I say something about Maya to make it even?"

"Do you like your nose the way it is?" I ask drily.

Ben snorts. "Are we done measuring our—"

"Liv!" Dom says. "What are you doing here?"

Olivia is standing in front of the table, hands on her hips, dressed in a white crop top and purple leggings. "Being compared to a gun apparently?"

"You caught that?" asks Miles.

"You talk loud," she retorts. "Look, Gia called to tell me we got an international email flagged as important. Our expansion plan worked, and the CEO of a medical technology company in Shanghai wants to invest and possibly merge a satellite office or two. They want to meet immediately, before the end of their workday."

"And you showed up here to tell me all that?" Dom asks.

"I called, but you didn't pick up, so I figured I should

track you down instead of hoping you'd eventually pick up the damn phone. We're running out of hours, and with the time difference…"

"Right, of course." Dom stands up, tossing a few Benjamins on the table. "That should cover drinks for the rest of the night. Gentlemen—"

"I should come with you," I say.

Olivia frowns. "Why?"

"I speak fluent Mandarin for starters. Learned it at Berkeley for international business. It's one of the foremost spoken languages in the world," I explain. "I know most of our clients speak English as well, but I've found it builds rapport to use both languages in negotiations if possible. Besides, I helped with the expansion proposal, and I would argue my contributions could be valuable."

"Fine," Dominic says. "Appreciate it. Since we royally pissed off the rest of the board, it would be a good strategy to try to earn their good graces back, wouldn't you say?"

Olivia nods. "Right. Of course."

"Should we head back to the Sterling building?" I ask.

"Liv has a home office we should be able to stream from. She was more savvy with working from home, so her set up is ideal, and probably a hell of a lot more organized than mine," Dom says, rubbing the back of his neck. "I'll admit the housekeeper has declared it no man's land there."

"I'm surprised she didn't have a heart attack even looking into the room," Olivia remarks. "Mom about died trying to do your laundry once."

Dom frowns at her. The scrunch of his face is quite possibly the most un-Dominic gesture I've seen lately. He's always stoic and reserved. "That's not true! Now you're just making stuff up."

"Am I?" She raises a brow.

"There's a reason I refused to room with you in college," I admit. "Dude, you were a *slob*. I mean, no one would know with the empire you've built for yourself, but seriously. I was worried we'd have to call a biohazard team."

"Anyway!" Dom claps his hands together. "Let's not forget I'm the boss of both of you. Let's get to Liv's before we lose the billion dollar clients."

I've never been to Olivia's apartment. I only know vaguely where she lives, but the second she texts me the address, I realize she's almost within walking distance of the bar. Convenient, all things considered.

It feels like an invasion to be here, but as we pull into the parking garage, one after the other like some kind of police escort, it's too late to back out now. Her place is much closer than the Sterling building, and admittedly, even though Dom owns the entire building, we don't own every floor, and the night security officers don't need to deal with the shock of the three of us turning up in the dead of night.

As we ride the elevator up to Olivia's penthouse, the terrible music fills the silence, but it doesn't make it any less awkward. She avoids eye contact with me as much as possible, looking down at the floor so our eyes don't meet in the reflection of the sliding door. When it finally opens and Olivia types the code in for her front door, I'm relieved to be able to put some physical space between us.

I know she heard Miles's comments but I'm not sure how long she was eavesdropping for. I don't want to undo all of the progress we've made towards peaceful coexistence, but I'm starting to realize that may not be possible. There's gasoline poured between us, and it feels like there's constantly an open flame just a few inches away. Combustion is almost inevitable.

Her apartment is surprisingly cozy. I know Dom's place looks like *Architectural Digest* threw up all over it, but the ultramodern, antiseptic look after the housekeeper finishes up his mess works for him... as opposed to the *Hoarders* look that would make even TLC audiences cringe.

My apartment is almost un-lived in, and he and I definitely have that in common, but Livvy has built a home here. There's tons of color and art surrounding us, and the antique furniture compliments all of the paintings perfectly. She's always been a collector, and her knick-knack collection proudly sits on display with her books and photos. The pastels around us make it warm and lively, and when a tiny Scottish fold cat tears around the corner and barrels into Dom's legs, I can't fight the laugh.

"Who is this?" I ask.

The cat hisses at me.

"Benedict Bridgerton," Olivia says. "Dom got him for me. Hence why he's Benedict's favorite."

Benedict eyes me with narrowed yellow eyes. Maybe he's figured out Olivia's feelings about me, because his gaze tells me everything I need to know. Most cats are a little standoffish at first, except when it comes to Dominic, who apparently is a cat whisperer and the exception to every rule.

"Benedict Bridgerton? I always thought you'd be more into the Duke," I reply. It's such an offhand comment that I don't think twice about it, but when Olivia's jaw hangs open like I've dropped a massive atomic bomb, I can't help but think twice about it.

Dom frowns. "Who?"

"You've watched *Bridgerton*?" Olivia gasps.

"Maya and I have sibling binge watching sessions once a month," I answer. "That was her pick. Believe me, I'd have preferred *Breaking Bad*."

"Mmhmm," Olivia says. "Admit it, it's addictive."

I shake my head. "If you say so."

"I know so," she replies.

"Maya has a list of shows we aren't allowed to watch together," Dom tells me. "Now I know why. It makes options limited when we're taking it easy after a long week."

"Too bad," I say, "Sibling privilege."

Her apartment is a decent size, especially for its location in the heart of the city. As we walk down the hallway past identical closed doors, I wonder how long she's lived here, how long it took to build a home. Admittedly, I'm shocked she doesn't have a boyfriend living here with her, but I shove that thought to the back of my mind.

Her home office has a certain academic charm to it; it belongs in a building at Yale, for sure. Vaulted ceilings, fire escape, giant Persian rug, first editions of classic literature bound in leather—it's almost too aesthetically pleasing to be real, but the computer monitors and antique filing cabinets left partially open tell me she spends enough time in this space.

"I'd work virtually all the time if I had an office like this," I say.

She blushes. "I wanted to make sure I had an oasis for when I take work home."

"You say that like you don't bring work home all the time," Dom chimes in.

"Alright, we better get to this meeting," Olivia says, holding up a hand to cut both of us off. "I have a TED talk to prepare."

"So you never did tell me much about the TED Talk thing. How'd that happen?"

She shrugs. "After they found out about my 30-under-30 Women In Tech award, TED reached out to me to talk about my experiences as a young, female CFO who runs a successful company with my brother."

TED Talks are one of those things everyone in the MBA program shoots for. Hell, I'd say a lot of high-strung Type As are always eagerly looking for a chance to humble brag in front of an audience. I never really thought much about it, but I know it's something Olivia would excel at, and pride blooms in my smile before I can second-guess it.

"I didn't get a TED Talk," Dom says. "Not gonna lie, I feel a little cheated."

"You get to be one of the youngest billionaires in the world," she retorts.

I didn't realize Dom had made it to that bracket, but it makes sense. Most of the time, my extra 0s go to a rotating list of charities, mostly because the thought of sitting on investments without any care for other people doesn't sit right with me. I think my mother would shun me if I turned into a wealthy asshole who owns a million country clubs.

I just figured Olivia would also match his salary. I mean, given the fact they're equals in the company, at least socially, it would make sense. But the way she's talking tells me that may not be the case, after all.

"And what about you?" I ask. "You aren't…?"

"I decline a salary increase every time Dom tries to raise it," she answers. "I have everything I need. So instead, we give employee bonuses and subsidize health insurance. Take care of our people, you know?"

"You've also had the same salary since the 2010s," Dom butts in. "I try every quarter, and she always declines and threatens to resign if I don't leave it be. I've been trying to get Maya on board with nagging her, but she's always saying I should respect her wishes."

"Again, everything I need," she says firmly. "Why are we so focused on my money?"

"Right. Shanghai."

We log into the meeting, and as we dive into semantics and translations to negotiate, I try my best to keep my head in the game. But it feels a little impossible, especially when I'm looking at her every second I can, sneaking glances like we're back in high school.

9

Olivia

Given the fact I spent so many of my younger years standing up in front of audiences, you would think I'd be used to the racing heart, the sweaty palms. It's impressive, the way I can shake off the eyes of hundreds of people and speak clearly, even when I'm so unsteady a strong breeze could knock me down.

My TED Talk is being delivered under harsh stage lights, in front of a live audience of far too many people for my liking, and with what feels like a million cameras capturing every possible angle of my face, I'm self-conscious enough about my outfit, possible pit stains, and whether or not I've developed a stress pimple of some kind.

Breathe, Liv, breathe.

Dom is on his way to sit backstage at my request. He and Maya got my two guest passes after Gia told me she couldn't make it out, and I keep nervously looking around to see if they've made it yet. When I see Alex first, confusion floods me, and with Dom behind him, I'm even more lost.

"Maya got held up at the airport coming back from her

speaking engagement and wanted me to come instead," he explains, before I can ask. "I can leave if you want."

Surprisingly, I don't want him to. Hell, I'm *relieved* he's here, and I'm not even sure why. Maybe it's the fact he's always had a calming presence. Maybe it's nostalgia. Either way, it's not my biggest concern at the moment.

"No, no," I say. "I'm glad you guys made it."

"You're going to be amazing, Liv," Dom tells me. "They picked you for a reason. There's no one in the world who deserves this more than you. Take your moment."

I nod. "I know I can do this, I just…"

"Just nothing," he says. "You have worked so hard for this moment, and it belongs to you and you alone. Get out there."

Alex smiles at me. He doesn't say a word, but the crinkling of his eyes makes me breathe a little steadier, and whatever worries I had melt away as Dom throws an arm around me and hugs me tightly. For a moment, I believe I can do anything.

The words are memorized after long weeks of practicing in the mirror, but my cue cards are sitting in my pocket anyway. As I stride across the floor, thankfully boot free, the audience roars with applause.

"My name is Olivia Sterling," I say with a smile. When my voice comes out even, measured as if I've never been nervous before in my life, I have to resist the urge to pump my fist in victory. *Okay, I've got this. Really got this.*

"I'm the Chief Financial Officer at Sterling Innovations, a medical technology development company based here in San Francisco. My brother and I founded Sterling by taking the bones off the hands of a CEO and owner we admired very much, and together, we rescued it from the brink of extinction… which I now realize makes it sound like an endangered species instead of a business, but I guess if you squint really hard, the logo looks like a zebra or something."

Thankfully, people laugh at my dumb joke. I'm so relieved I don't know what to do with myself.

"Recently, I got an email that changed my life. You know all of those videos of kids getting excited about their dream colleges? Yeah, that was sort of me." I pause. "The 30-Under-30 Women in Technology event has honored me as their Woman of the Year and spokesperson, and if I'd told myself a few years ago that I'd be able to say those words, I think I would've fainted."

"There aren't words for the immeasurable gratitude I feel, but I'll have to find them, because that's a speech I'll have to give *very* soon."

Once I'm a minute in, the rest of it is easy. I expected more of a challenge moving forward, but once I settle into the rhythm and cadence I need, it flows out of me with ease. I tried to write the presentation with the idea of what I might've needed to hear when I was a teenage girl pursuing business and a freshman at an Ivy League College with some of the most hostile competition I've ever known. What did I need to know? How was I going to survive? All of those questions fueled me moving forward, and it would've been easier had someone sat me down and given me wisdom.

So I try to give my past self what I needed in the span of a fifteen minute conversation. I keep wondering if I'm gonna slip up and trip over my words, but when I finally reach the conclusion of my speech, I feel perfectly grounded, the whole room engrossed in what I have to say and at attention. It's nice, given how rarely it happens everywhere else around the male assholes I have to deal with.

The amount of times a visiting client has mistaken me

as a secretary might be enough to make someone else want to quit, but I know I'm made of tougher stuff, and at this point in my career, I don't have to prove anything to anyone. I know my place. I know where I stand. I know what I've earned.

I slowly walk across the stage to deliver my final words, taking my time to make sure they resonate, that if nothing else from tonight is heard, they are; "All I have left to say is this: to all the girls out there who think the highest towers are for boys, climb anyway. If you think your dreams are too big, dream bigger. And when someone tells you that you can't do something because you're a girl, do it anyway. You will always be your biggest champion."

Saying the final words is almost too good to be true.

"Thank you for coming to my TED Talk."

I practically float off the stage as the lights dim. It's unreal, the elation I feel at this moment. I feel like I could do just about anything, and as I think about the mental checklist I have of career bucket list moments, I realize I've just crossed one off.

This. Is. Fucking. Awesome.

"I can't believe I just did that!" I exclaim, jumping up and down. I feel a little silly doing it, but the giddiness is almost too much for me to contain. "I just gave a TED Talk!"

"Alright," Dom says, wrapping me in a bear hug. "Cool it for a minute. I'm sure there are a bunch of camera people and audience members who are ready to ambush you on the way out, so be ready for that. After all the speeches you're making this year, you're going to be pretty famous."

He's right. I've never been as high profile as he is—especially after he made *People's* 'Sexiest Men Alive' spread. It's a good laugh now, but at the time, he was so confused by the sudden friend requests and follows that he deleted his social media profiles for an indefinite hiatus. Dom is the extrovert of the two of us, and he's always been better at handling the attention we get.

Me? I'm a disaster and a half most of the time when it comes to this sort of thing. I don't know how to do PR or choose the right headshots, and the idea of trying to do a lot of those things feels like being a trained monkey in a circus.

But I'm not gonna let it bring me down right now. All I need to do is think about what's in front of me.

Dinner, drinks, celebration. That's all I need.

Alex leans down, his lips dangerously close to brushing my ear. His voice is low, and the sound of it causes goosebumps to raise on my arms. His proximity is dizzying. It shouldn't be, given that he's a coworker, and maybe a friend. I don't know why I'm so flustered, but I am.

"Congratulations," he says. "You did great."

"Thanks," I tell him.

Walking to the car through the back door means some of the foot traffic is lighter, but not by much. There are still plenty of people demanding my attention, and too many cameras with the flash on trying to snap a photo of the Sterling siblings. Dom keeps his relationship on the down low, and as far as the press is concerned, he's a single man with cash to spend and a good relationship with his family. Throw in a few photos, and he's a cash cow for gold diggers everywhere.

The second we're in the safety of Dom's Tesla, I breathe a sigh of relief. The tinted windows give me some degree of privacy, and after the insane performance I just gave and the stimuli hitting me like a truck, I need a second to breathe.

"Does this mean I need to hire someone to maintain a public social media presence?" I joke.

"Maya knows everything about that stuff," Alex chimes in. "But it's nothing you need to worry about right now. You're a woman in STEM, not a Kardashian."

Dom nods. "Besides, the work you're doing is changing the world. You don't need instagram sponsors to make your way. You're already there."

He squeezes my shoulder briefly before he returns his hands to the wheel. I'm suddenly so aware that Alex is a few feet away in the backseat, and I can smell his aftershave and woodsy cologne as the air blasts through the vents. When I peek in the rearview, I see his face, thumbing through his phone.

"So where is our dinner reservation?" asks Alex.

"The four-star Sushi place by the Wharf," Dom answers. "It's Liv's favorite. They have karaoke in the bar, her favorite Saké, and it's low key enough that we can eat in peace."

"More like I can share a meal with *you* in peace. Since you're Mr. Popular and all," I correct him. "Anyway, is Maya going to make it?"

"She's meeting us there. She just texted - her flight just got in," Alex says.

I frown. "Are we okay to bring four people?"

"I made a reservation for five," Dom chuckles. "I wasn't sure who would make the guest list. Wanted to play it safe."

That sounds like my brother. He never leaves anything unaccounted for. I know life is what happens when you're busy making plans, but Dom is the type of guy who seems to always expect the unexpected and land on his feet. I mean, maybe it's just a CEO thing.

I remember very vividly I used to have to tie Dom's chopsticks together with a rubber band when we'd eat

Japanese food. He had no idea how to use them, and even with my help, he was resisting the temptation to ask for a fork. Eventually, he figured it out. He might have launched a few pieces of spicy tuna across the restaurant, but now, he can use his own chopsticks without my help or hairbands.

Alex never liked sushi when we were younger, but he loves ramen. At least, I assume he does, if his palate hasn't been refined by expensive tastes. All I know is that people change the way the leaves on the trees fall, the way the seasons slip into each other. I used to have him memorized. Now, he's a blank page.

I thought it would be weird, having Alex here. Weirdly though, after I got off the TED stage and met him and Dom behind the curtains, it felt right to have him there. I was relieved to see him, even though I wasn't expecting it. Part of me is glad that Dom brought him instead of Maya, and part of me is mad that neither of them asked me beforehand, and another part is just grateful and enjoying the moment.

"You okay?" Dom asks, as he holds the door open to the restaurant.

"Yeah," I say. "I can't believe I'm gonna be thirty soon, and already I've... I feel like I..."

"Hey," Alex cuts in. "Livvy, you brilliant woman. You think too big and too far ahead. Be in this moment, your moment."

I don't know exactly *when* it happened, but I realize I'm not looking at him the same. There's no disdain or hate clouding my judgment. Instead of assuming the worst of him, trying to figure out what he could be getting at, I finally feel like, maybe, he's actually being sincere.

For the first time in a long time, I'm listening to Alex. Really listening. And I'm realizing how much he cares about me, in irrefutable evidence. I used to get overwhelmed a lot when I was younger, and he was always there to talk me down and make the world feel just a little bit smaller.

I'm thinking about Alex too often now that I have to see him every day. Nostalgia is fine, but tripping down the slippery slope that leads to feelings is not something I have time for. Or energy. Or really anything at all. If I give it too much thought, I'm screwed.

"I need to run to the restroom," I announce. "Order a bottle for the table, Dom?"

I make a beeline for the ladies' room, desperate to splash some water on my face and cool off. The memories flooding my mind are quick, flashing through the greatest hits of Alex and me until I finally come to my senses.

Take a breath.

We're getting dangerously close to the awards ceremony and I still haven't found an alternate date for Alex. Not that he doesn't deserve to go, but I'm afraid of the implications, afraid of the fact I want him to be there. I just don't know what else we'd do for that second charity date, and the clock is ticking.

And I'm thinking about way too many things at once. Problems and solutions are easier to figure out when they aren't accompanied by an army of other concerns. I try to breathe, bracing myself against the sink, the water dripping down my face.

This is my day, and theoretically, this should be the moment I let it all go, eat my weight in sushi, enjoy a few drinks, and pretend I'm not shamelessly thirsting over my ex-boyfriend because it's been a criminally long time since I got laid.

When I arrive back at the table, Maya, Gia, Dom, and Alex have already made themselves comfortable.

"Maya called," Gia says brightly. "Said I could show up fashionably late. How does it feel to be a sexy TED Talker?"

I laugh. "A sexy one, huh?"

"A lot of them are old and crusty," she says with a shrug. "You're a knockout. You'll go viral so fast. Just wait."

Dom chuckles. "Maybe Gia should be your social media manager."

"You need one?" Gia asks.

Maya rolls her eyes. "Don't hold your breath, Gia. These two are allergic to technology."

"Ironic, given what Sterling does," Alex remarks.

It's nice being here, all together and laughing like there's nothing in the world to worry about. It feels like being normal twentysomethings, rather than the faces behind one of the most successful tech companies in the world. I know I have a lot going for me, and all things considered, I'm doing well, but unfortunately, anxiety doesn't listen to reason, and for every good moment, there are a million worries in my busy head. Occasionally, I need these happy moments so I can pretend my life is a sitcom and not a pressure cooker.

Breathe, Liv, breathe.

10

Alex

"It was an amazing speech!" Dom says as Olivia recounts her TED Talk.

She likes to gloss over all the details, but it's not a false humility. For her, it's a genuine focus on her work or philanthropy rather than personal gain. Some would be concerned with building a platform, but her? She cares more about making an impact, changing the world.

She may be stubborn and push all of my buttons, but she's something special.

I just wish she could see that. Isn't that always how it goes, though? The best people can't acknowledge just how special they are.

"And she's gonna kick ass *again* at the awards ceremony," Gia gushes. "You're going with her, right?"

She's talking to *me*. That fact registers a few seconds too late, and I find myself searching my brain, wondering if I somehow missed the invitation.

"I wasn't aware that I was invited," I say with a frown.

"That's the whole reason she went to the auction,

right?" Gia nudges Olivia. "Didn't you go to find some arm candy for the ceremony?"

"Well, yeah, but..." Her cheeks flush red. "I need another drink."

She walks across the restaurant to the bar, and Gia's eyes shift in her direction. When she purses her lips, gesturing with her eyebrows for me to follow her, I take the cue and excuse myself from the table for another old fashioned.

"So when were you going to ask me to come to your special night?" I murmur, standing closer to her so she can hear me over the noise of the bar and the terrible karaoke in the corner. Her perfume hits me first, and I can see the corner of her eyes where her mascara is starting to smear after a long day. Even under her foundation, I can see the freckles on the bridge of her nose.

Isn't it weird how someone can still have power over you, even after years apart? How strange is that?

"I mean, I just hadn't brought it up yet." She glances at me, biting down on her lower lip. "I guess, for the second date, do you want to..."

"Sure," I say. "Where's the ceremony?"

I know I have to play this cool, be as delicate as possible to avoid seeming too eager to see her. Of course I want to see her, be around her, but I haven't figured out what that even means yet. To be honest, there's a lot I haven't figured out.

"San Diego."

"When?" I ask.

"The weekend after next."

"I wouldn't miss it for the world."

"You're not obligated to come," she says quickly. "Seriously. I know it's kind of unconventional and not really what you signed up for with the auction—"

"It's important to you," I interrupt. "That's all I need. Besides, after the TED Talk you just gave, I'm excited to see how you top it."

"You really liked it?" she asks.

"How could I not?"

"Alex…" she says quietly. Her cheeks are flushed from her drinks, and her eyes are shining, and when she looks at me, I realize how little space there is between us. How easy it would be to close that space.

I'm not gonna kiss her. Not here, anyway, not when her brother is still at the table and the room is full of people and I'm not positive she won't slap me into next week if I tried it. I want to kiss her when she wants it, when I know I can breathe her in and not come up for air, when I can drown in the taste of her.

I wonder if she still tastes like honey. So sweet it's almost unreal.

"It's getting late," I say, clearing my throat. I step back from her, and my whole body feels like lead pinned against the floor. Somehow, I put distance between us. Somehow, I pull back from her.

"I'm gonna call an Uber and head home," she says, looking down at her phone. "Got a bunch of meetings tomorrow."

"Yeah, me too."

I don't. I don't know why I say that when it's not true, but I can't seem to remember how to speak, and every nerve in my body is alive, roaring with passion, desperate to take her in my arms and cross all the lines we've carefully put between us.

I can't kiss her. As much as I want to. As much as I wish it was as easy as that. Nothing is simple, nothing is *ever* that simple.

"I, uh, I'll wait with you," I say.

Livvy grabs her purse and says goodbye to the rest of the table. Gia, Dom, and Maya decide to head out at the same time, so the five of us are outside of the bar for a few moments while the valet brings Dom's car back around.

"My Uber is five minutes out," Livvy says.

"Ten," I reply, holding up my phone.

She sighs, leaning her head back. "The cool air feels nice. It was so stuffy in there." She glances over at me, her hair falling in loose, messy waves down past her shoulders. It reminds me of when we'd head to the beach, how she'd let the wind unravel the curls she meticulously placed and let her hair be wild. I love her wild hair. She has a lioness mane, the kind of hair a guy could get lost in when kissing her.

She glances at me. "Hey, Alex?"

"Yeah, Livvy?"

Her cheeks bloom with scarlet at the nickname. "I've really liked hanging out with you."

"I've liked hanging out with you too."

She takes a breath, nodding her head. I glance away from her, checking the Uber app before I've officially been looking at her for far too long to be a fleeting thing, a purely professional relationship. My blood is rushing in my ears, and my thoughts are drifting very quickly out of safe for work territory, and I'm consumed by the war between my mind and my body, which want two very different things.

We've long since watched Maya, Dom, and Gia ride off and away from the bar, and now that we're alone, really alone, the energy has shifted. There's a charge in the air, like lightning in a storm.

"Alex," she says again.

I look at her, and the second I turn, she's got her hands on the collar of my suit jacket, and she's kissing me. She's kissing me with her lips tasting like the sugar rim of her cocktail glass, strawberry chapstick, and something that's entirely just *Olivia*.

I am kissing Olivia Sterling.

It takes me a few fractions of a second to realize the meaning of those five words. The second I register her lips against mine, soft and sweet as I remember, I kiss her back. I let instinct take over, my hands grasping her face, sliding in the front strands of her hair and pushing them back, tangling myself in her until our bodies have closed any gaps between us. She moans, her tongue sliding into my mouth, and I forget all reason, all sense. I just devour her, letting her burn me from the inside out, like a fine whiskey.

Her hands trail down my chest and then back up, around my shoulders, against the scruff of my jaw, into the curls at the nape of my neck. She's everywhere, in my bones, in the tap of my heart against my ribs.

Fucking hell. It's just as amazing as I thought it would be.

I didn't know how much I missed her, missed *this*, until this moment. Now that I'm touching her, feeling her silhouette pressed against me, tasting every inch of her perfect mouth, I feel like a space I didn't know was empty has been filled, and it's exhilarating. This kiss. This moment. This woman.

A car horn honks, pulling us out of the moment. I'm reminded that we're standing in the middle of San Francisco and making out on the street like a couple of horny teenagers, and I pull back from her reluctantly, the taste of her still on my tongue.

"That's my Uber," she says sheepishly. "I'll, uh, see you at work tomorrow."

I can't tell you what I thought about the entire drive home from the bar. When I got through my front door,

Bidding on Love

enjoying the greeting from my dogs and their happy barks, she's in my mind as clear as a photograph.

Maybe I'm a dead man for even thinking about her this way. Maybe this is all going to crash and burn, but I'm drunk on her and I don't even care. The consequences can wait. The whole world can wait. I'm going to enjoy this cloud nine for as long as I can ride it out.

It turns out the consequences only wait for a matter of hours. The second Maya and I are alone in her tiny office the next morning, going over dinner plans with my mom, she takes one look at me and demands that I tell her exactly what I did the night before.

"You look way too happy," she says. "What? Did you get laid or something?"

"No," I reply incredulously. "And even if I did, would you really want to know?"

She shakes her head. "Probably not."

"Exactly."

"Something did happen, though," she says, her eyes narrowed. Maya has always had this keen ability to sniff people out. When we were kids, it was ammunition for her own blackmailing purposes (usually to sit shotgun or have first dibs on the TV).

"Will you drop it?" I ask.

Maya narrows her eyes. "You're testy today. What, did you and Olivia rip each other a new one again?" She pauses. "No, not that. But I'm close, aren't I? Did something happen between you two?"

I avoid her stare, trying to think of a good change of subject as fast as possible. "Maya—"

"Alejandro!" she exclaims. "Tell me you didn't make a move on her."

I sigh. "It's not like that. I just… We were waiting for our rides and we kissed."

"YOU DID WHAT?" she shrieks.

"Shhh!" I say, glancing around nervously. The door is shut, but the walls are thin in this office, and I've had enough drama since I started here to last me until retirement. "She kissed me. I kissed her back. It's no big deal."

"IT'S A MASSIVE FUCKING DEAL!" Maya exclaims.

"Would you lower your voice? Please?"

She nods, quieting down. "Dominic is going to kill you."

"That's exactly why he can never find out," I say. "It was a lapse in judgment."

"I knew you looked too cozy at the bar with her."

Normally I'd tell her she was reading too much into it. That the room was dark and the music was loud and we were all drinking. Something out of nothing. Except it's not something out of nothing at all, because a harmless interaction became a kiss.

"Maya, please."

"I'm not gonna say anything to Dom, but what were you thinking, Alex? She's hated you forever, and you broke her heart and probably are the reason she's sworn off men for the last decade, not to mention you work together and she's your best friend's *sister*. You couldn't have made out with anyone else? Seriously?"

"She kissed me first."

"I'm sure the eyes you were making at her were so one-sided then," Maya deadpans. "Look, Alex, I know you two have a history and I know she's gorgeous and you're both consenting adults, but you don't shit where you eat."

"You're dating the CEO of the company," I point out.

"Yeah, well, we didn't have an ugly breakup as teenagers that caused a falling out for years and almost compromised an important business relationship, made the entire office uncomfortable, and had everyone in the entry-level positions betting on who would quit first."

When simplified like that, I definitely see exactly where I fucked up. I see it a little too well, and as much as I hate to admit it, Maya is right. I can't tell her that, of course, because she has a tendency to never let me hear the end of it when I give her an inch, but she's definitely made me think twice.

It was easy not to think about the past when Olivia and I never spoke to each other. It was even harder to keep my head on straight when there was a lot more distance there. I can't go back and undo the kiss, but I definitely need to be careful how I move forward right now.

Because this? This will get ugly. And I'm not 100% sure whether or not Dom will kill me. I'm pretty sure he'll punch my lights out, but if I piss Olivia off, she might do the same, and he taught her how to throw her left hook.

"I want you to be happy, I do, but are you really thinking this through?" she asks. "Yeah, it would be great if you could be friends again and get along in the workplace, but what happens if it ends the same way? Sterling needs you on the Board, and Dom needs Olivia to run the place. Besides, she's my friend, and she doesn't need to get hurt again."

"Then I'll figure out how to keep it professional," I say. *While on a date hundreds of miles away with a hotel room, no responsibilities, and more drinks? How the fuck am I going to keep my cool then?*

"I don't think it's that easy," she replies. "But anyway,

Dom is gonna be in any minute, and so is Liv, so you need to put your game face on."

I take a gulp of my coffee, immediately wishing it was something stronger. "Take Liv's latte. Please."

"You got her a latte?" Maya raises her eyebrows.

"I don't need to hear it," I say.

"Okay, okay."

Olivia is standing in her office when I step out of Maya's and start walking towards the conference room for my first strategy meeting with Dom. He's usually running late after a night out, so it doesn't surprise me that I'm here first.

She's got her hair up today, falling elegantly around one of her signature claw-clips. It's easygoing without being lazy, and it suits her outfit well. I try not to check her out, even though the temptation hits me hard. I find myself at war, wondering if I should talk to her, if I'd be better off keeping my distance instead of sticking my neck out.

When I catch her eyes, she stops in the doorway, closes her fingers around the knob, and slams it shut.

Hard.

Right. So that's where we're at with each other.

11

Olivia

I have this thing.

Okay, so it's not really a thing. Or maybe it is. I have a bit of a complex when it comes to intimacy, or rather, vulnerability. Whenever I'm on a date that gets a little too real, where I open up a little too much, I turn into the ghost of a romantic's past and disappear off the face of the Earth. After sex, I march out of his bed before he can even throw the condom away. I don't stay, I don't make the first move, and I certainly don't entertain romantic notions about Alex Hernandez.

Except I decided to break every single rule in the book last night outside of that bar, and I'm not 100% sure it won't happen again. It can't happen again for a laundry list of reasons, the least of which being we work together, but for every logical explanation for why I'm the biggest idiot on the planet, there are a hundred more thoughts in my head about how strong he is, how good he feels, how much I love the scratch of his jaw and what that jaw might feel like in other places…

Dangerous. Train. Of. Thought.

He kissed me back. I know that to be an unequivocal truth, though I can't decide if it makes the situation better or worse. If he'd pushed me away, I could say it was the drinks that made me stupid and the whole thing was a humiliating mistake. But he didn't push me away, and the fact he didn't push me away means he wanted to kiss me too.

And if he wanted to kiss me too, well, we're doomed.

Maybe we were both drunk. Maybe we were both confused. Maybe I tripped and he tripped and his tongue accidentally fell into my mouth or mine into his. Happens all the time, right? It's an easy thing to explain away and dismiss and forget about, right? I know I should be smart enough to figure out what to do in this situation, but my mind is wiped blank.

I want to tell him it can't happen again, that it was a mistake. I want to write it off as something I never would consider doing sober, but the worst part about being sober is that my feelings are much clearer, *sharper*. In the light of the morning, I want to kiss him again. I want to do more than kiss him again.

Remember what he did, Liv.

Took my virginity. Ran out on me. Those are horrible things, and especially in my teenage mind, they were treasonous offenses I could never get past. But this isn't the same Alex, just like I'm not the same Olivia. It's not as simple as an adolescent grudge. The Alex I'm getting to know is smart, understanding, works hard, and loves rescue dogs enough to endure a date with me trying to bite his head off constantly so he can donate to charity. That's an Alex I'm attracted to for who he is, and it's not helpful that he's aged like a fine wine, either. Maybe if he were ugly, this would be easier.

Why couldn't he fall victim to male pattern baldness? I

thought wronging a woman meant losing one's hair younger. How does he still have a full head of gorgeous, wonderful, pullable hair?

OLIVIA!

I'm losing my mind. I must be. I'm thinking about pulling Alex's hair, and I'm remembering past times I've pulled his hair and now I'm wondering how much he's improved since then and holy shit, I'm officially down the rabbit hole. Call me Alice.

When he walks out of Maya's office, his ass tight in his black trousers, his shoes immaculate, warm leather, his muscles flexing under his suit jacket as his watch catches the light, I steal too many looks. I take all of him in. I think about things I shouldn't think about, and I start to blush.

And then, like he's got some kind of ESP for my reactions, he turns to look at me.

I slam the door shut quickly.

It was probably the least smooth move I could make, but I'm freaking out, and I have no idea what to say to him. He's the kind of guy who communicates well. He likes to talk things out, get to the bottom of it. Me? I'd rather not. I don't know what to say, and I don't trust myself not to start blurting out a million embarrassing things the second I get nervous.

I didn't used to feel nervous around him, but suddenly, he's reduced me to a shut-in who'd rather hide in my office than navigate a conversation with the dude I made out with last night.

I like him.

That's the problem.

I like him sober, I like him even when I'm pissed off, and I like him even when I remember how he did me dirty when we were younger. I like him despite all of the reasons

I shouldn't, and I feel like the biggest fool in the entire world.

I should hate him. It was easier to hate him.

Normally, this is the kind of thing I would tell Dom about, but he's far too protective over me, and the last thing I need is for him to throw punches at his best friend just because he's defending my honor like this is some kind of duel. I'm a grown woman, and I should be able to decide my next move.

But my heart and my mind are at war.

And I just signed up for a trip away with him.

I have an Ivy League education and a decent head on my shoulders. Theoretically, I should be able to let logic run the show, but theory is useless in this scenario, because something about Alex makes my brain melt faster than a popsicle in the summertime.

I don't know how I manage to get through my work day, but I do. It's a difficult balance, sleuthing around to make sure he's not in a room I need to enter, avoiding him and Maya at every possible moment to make sure we're not left alone to talk about The Incident. Calling it The Incident makes me feel like I'm referring to some kind of spec ops mission gone terribly wrong, but even referencing last night as a kiss makes me blush so much I can't tone it down.

The more distance I can put between myself and those feelings, the better.

I'm lucky that my feelings about Alex and my worry doesn't interfere with doing my job, because I have every fear that I'll spiral out and start to slack off if I get too involved with dating. The reason I'm excellent at what I do is that I never let anything else be my top priority. Dating opens the door to making things messy and shifting my priorities around. I used to be good at pushing it out of my mind, but lately, all bets are off.

My usual tricks didn't work all day. The second my mind started to wander, he was there in the back of it. When I had downtime between meetings or analytics or the million other tasks on my calendar, even if it was just a minute, I thought about his kiss. By the time five o'clock rolled around, I was so ready to leave that nothing else mattered.

Most of the time, I'm not out the door before seven pm at the earliest. Neither is Dom, and sometimes, he even stays later. Hell, the couch in his office pulls out into a bed. But, when Mom declares it's family dinner time, we come to family dinner at precisely six sharp.

Neither of us have ever been late to family dinner, but I think it's safe to assume tardiness would warrant being smacked in the ass with Mom's broom because we're "never too big for a whooping." I'd like to avoid that fate.

Dad has decided that decent weather means it's time to clean out the freezer full of meat and spend his afternoon smoking it in the yard. When I pull up to our home: a modest two-story in Sunset Hills, I can already smell Dad cooking. When our company made it big, we offered to buy our parents a new house, but they refused, saying that this was their home. They did compromise and let us pay to remodel it, though.

Things were a little tight growing up from time to time. I know my mom still feels guilty sometimes about not being able to afford my insulin when I ran out before insurance authorized refills, but we're closer than ever these days. All of that is water under the bridge.

"Olivia!" Mom is the first one to greet me when I walk

through the door, squeezing me so tightly I hold my breath until she lets go. "You look beautiful today!"

Mom is a lot shorter than me, especially when she's not wearing heels. I got Dad's height, and so did Dom, who towers over just about everyone. We have the same caramel hair, hers streaked with gray, and our eyes, which are identical hues of green, are only differentiated by the laugh lines at the corner of hers.

She's currently wearing a "Proud Yale Mom" crewneck sweatshirt I bought her years ago, and a pair of blue jeans with her feet bare. She studied at Berkeley and embraced the barefoot hippie aesthetic during her Woodstock days. Even now, the free-spirit in her definitely comes through. I think she's where I get my passion from. Dad always says I got her mouth.

I laugh. "Mom, I just got off of work. This is what I look like every day."

"Well, everyone says we look alike, so when I compliment you, I compliment me too," she says with a wink. "Here, help me carry out the appetizers. We're eating out on the deck."

"Is Dom here yet?" I ask.

"Oh, yeah, he and Maya are almost here and Alma is outside already. Alex should be on his way too." She speaks so matter-of-factly, as if this is a conversation we've already had and not the first time I'm hearing of her plans. Knowing her, she probably forgot to mention it. That, or she's been scheming. Maybe both.

I pause. "Did you say…"

"The Hernandez family is joining us for dinner," Mom says slowly. Like I heard her wrong.

"Why?" I ask, frowning. "I thought this was a family dinner."

"We always had family dinners together growing up,"

she replies. "Besides, now that Maya and Dom are seeing one another, it seems only right that we all get together. The four of you are working together, anyhow. I don't see how having dinner together is any different."

I never told anyone the specifications of what went down between Alex and I. Sure, our parents were rooting for us, and everyone was a little disappointed that we couldn't make it work, but I managed to skate by under the guise of being heartbroken, and then when we grew into busy adults, it became easy to stay separate.

"Mom, I was kind of hoping for time with you and Dad. And Dom, I guess. But I didn't think we'd be having company."

She rolls her eyes. "Honey, I love you, but you have to stop avoiding our friends because you and Alex had a hard break-up. Sit on opposite ends of the table, for all I care. But we are having this dinner, and I don't care if I have to drag you outside myself."

Mom never yells. Sometimes I wish she was the type to yell at us, but instead, she's quiet and firm. Her word is final, and she doesn't have to raise her voice to make it very clear what we're supposed to be doing. When Dom and I would get on her nerves, she would only have to give us *the look* to make sure we changed our tune and started acting right.

Nothing puts the fear of god in you like your mother, that's for sure. I don't know what it is about her, but she has a way of changing anyone's tune.

I know better than to argue. I also know if I try to say anything about Alex, she's going to realize it's not a matter of hating each other or being at odds for petty reasons. No, it's about unresolved romantic tension, and my mother has a no-nonsense attitude about communication. Feelings need to be shared, otherwise, other people don't need to be burdened with the consequences of keeping everything internalized. Her words—albeit paraphrased—not mine.

Alma gives me a hug the second she sees me, and for a moment, I can almost pretend I'm not stressing over Alex or whatever strange things are happening between us. Of course, that relief only lasts for so long, because when he walks through the back door with Dom and Maya in tow, I take on a deer-in-the-headlights look about me.

"Hey, everybody!" he says, all easygoing, untouchable. He's changed into jeans and undone a few of the buttons of his shirt, and the way his hair is mussed is sinfully handsome. His eyes meet mine for a second before his mom brings him in for a hug, and my dad starts arguing with him about whether or not the Giants are gonna make the World Series this year.

Maya beams at me. "Olivia! I was hoping I could talk to you about something real quick. Can I borrow you?"

Thank fuck. I'd like to get out of here. "Yeah, uh, sure—"

"There's nothing you need to talk to Olivia about," Alex cuts in. "Right?"

Maya glares at him, and I'm left standing there with no idea what to say. I definitely feel like I'm missing a memo here, but I doubt anything is going to be said outright. It feels like when we were kids making up languages to speak in code around our parents.

"What?" I say. "What are you talking about, Alex?"

"But I think I *should* talk to Liv," Maya says pointedly, eyeing him.

"We worked it out already," he snaps. "Okay?"

"What is happening here?" Dom asks, at a loss as he cracks his beer open. "Did I miss something?"

"Nothing!" Maya and Alex exclaim in unison.

Cool, so Alex told Maya what happened.

"We'll talk later, Maya," I say, ignoring Alex entirely.

I don't know if she can keep a secret, but it doesn't matter, because I assumed he'd have the sense to keep our business between us. What a fucking asshole.

Alex opens his mouth to say something, but I walk away like I didn't notice. It's the only thing I can do to stay sane. Thankfully, our parents are engrossed in their own conversations, because the last thing I need is the Spanish Inquisition about the situation when I'm not even sure what's happening.

I used to love my job because it was uncomplicated. I understood the ins and outs, I could figure out what my day would look like before I even got out of bed. Now, it's all a wild card.

I have to resist the urge to smack him, and instead, I grit my teeth and smile so aggressively my jaw clicks. I focus my attention on Mom and Alma, doing everything I can to put physical distance between Alex and I. I don't trust my face not to reveal everything I'm feeling right now, and honestly, I'm not entirely sure where my head is at either.

This is going to be the longest family dinner of my entire life.

12

Alex

If looks could kill, I'd be so dead. And then probably brought back to life so Livvy could kill me again.

I always thought that phrase was kind of stupid, but after the last few weeks of dealing with the unbelievable tension between Olivia and me, I've started to understand it a little too well.

By the time we get to the end of dinner, I'm pretty sure Olivia has planned a hundred different ways to confront me, Maya is trying to figure out how to insert herself into the situation and fix everything, and Dom is completely oblivious to all of it. Knowing Olivia, she's thought the argument through and won it in her head already. Before the words are even said, she's mapped it out.

I can only imagine what's waiting for me if I can actually talk to her. All day I've been trying to catch her, but she's been dodging me like it's an Olympic sport. I know we have to talk eventually, especially because the very nature of our job is collaborative, but I'd rather it be sooner than later. Between the upcoming date, the meetings, and the fact our families seem hellbent on returning to old traditions, it's better to get it out of the way now.

So, when Olivia heads inside to run to the bathroom, I wait at the base of the stairs for her to get back.

She nearly jumps out of her skin when she sees me, stifling a yelp. "What the hell are you doing?"

"Waiting for you," I say. "I've been trying to talk to you."

"We don't have anything to talk about," she replies coolly.

"Oh, we don't?" I raise a brow, shaking my head. "So the kiss was nothing then? Never happened?"

My voice is a lot sharper than I mean for it to be, but between the cold shoulder and my sister, my patience has gotten very thin. I don't know what else to do, how to approach the situation. At this point, I'm just taking initiative, because sometimes with Olivia, it's like arguing with a goddamn brick wall.

Her eyes widen. "What the fuck, Alex?" She lowers her voice. "You really want to do this now? When anyone can just walk in?"

She raises a point. I can hear everyone laughing on the patio, but the door is unlocked, and I'm sure anyone else could head this way and overhear everything. Both of us come from nosy families, and the last thing I want is to deal with a barrage of questions I don't have answers for. Dom and his father both will have thoughts about me even *thinking* about pursuing Olivia again, and I'd rather not deal with that.

"You won't talk to me otherwise," I quip. "I figured I should just take the opportunity."

"Not here," she says at last. "Come on."

She leads me to her childhood bedroom, and I'm suddenly struck by the memory of her sneaking me up here when we were teenagers. Our parents probably knew exactly what we were up to, and they definitely weren't born yesterday, but we snuck around anyway like we had no other choice. My parents divorced when I was young and my dad wasn't around, but my mom stepped in and talked to me about all things sex and relationships. She bought my first box of condoms, and Olivia's mom took her to the clinic for birth control early on, but there was something so quintessentially young about sneaking into her bedroom.

It felt like a movie back then. Even now, it kind of does.

The bedroom has turned into a guest room and storage space since she moved out. The only relics from when Olivia occupied this space are the glow in the dark stars on the ceiling and the purple curtains. Most everything has been replaced or put into storage, but if I focus enough, I can remember everything about this place.

The fact that the grown up versions of the two crazy kids in love now find themselves in the same room, wondering what an impulsive kiss means, feels a little too symmetrical. Life has a funny way of working out like that.

"You couldn't have kept it to yourself, Alex?" she demands, the second the door closes behind us. "You had to go and blab to your sister? Before even talking to me? She's in a relationship with my brother, you idiot. What happens when she tells him?"

"She said she wouldn't say anything," I reply. "I didn't even tell her. She put it together on her own. Believe me, I'm the one risking a broken nose here. If I was going to tell someone, it wouldn't have been Maya. I didn't exactly have a choice."

I don't know if she believes me. Hell, I don't even know if it matters. She seems like she's already made up her mind about me, deciding that I'm some kind of traitor looking for a challenge or a quick lay. I don't know where she got these ideas about me, but I can see them written all over her face.

"Whatever," she says. "She knows. It's not a big deal, right?"

"Shouldn't be," I agree. "Maya respects us enough to keep it to herself. The last thing she wants is to piss Dom off, and she understands how important we are to the company. Work comes first."

"Work does come first," Olivia says. She chews her lip, her brows knitted together in the center of her forehead. Her frown forms the most adorable crease above her nose, and if I could, I'd kiss that look off of her.

"Look, I'm sorry I kissed you." I don't know if it's even true, but I say it anyway. "I know our working relationship is the priority, and I shouldn't have… It was a line, and I crossed it."

"I crossed it first," she admits. "We were drinking, it was stupid. An accident, right?"

"Yeah," I say. "And it won't happen again."

"Course not," she says with a scoff. Her voice squeaks a bit, wavering for all of a moment. "We can just keep this professional. Be strangers. Be islands, or whatever, once the date is over."

Thankfully, her avoiding me has given me the opportunity to think about what I have to say. She has a way of rendering me speechless, and with one piercing look, my mind goes blank, and suddenly, I'm a teenage boy fumbling through his words again. I have a line to walk, but I'm not ready to undo the progress we've made.

"We can't just ignore each other," I tell her. "I don't want to go back to how things were, when we weren't speaking and couldn't get along for more than a few seconds. We're going to be collaborating long term, and there's no use in pretending we can just get rid of each other anytime soon."

"I don't want to get rid of you," she says quietly.

I pause, reeling for a moment. The way she softens, the way the confession escapes her, it throws me off. Whatever anger she was carrying melts away, and what's left is a quiet, avoidant version of Livvy who can't seem to meet my eyes.

"You really hurt me back then, you know?" she finally says. "I mean, we had sex and then I thought maybe you were pulling a Miles or something. I felt so used and disgusted and I just…" She trails off.

Maybe I should've guessed that she felt that way a long time ago. I probably could've put the pieces together, but guessing her emotional state is a hell of a lot different than hearing it. I suppose we never did have the follow-up conversation, the *why?* now that the *why?* doesn't matter anymore.

I start, "I can explain—"

"Don't," she says. "Please. The whole thing was forever ago and it's embarrassing enough as it is. We don't have to talk about it. It's not even really the point."

"So what is the point?"

"I don't hate you, Alex. That's the problem," she says. "It was easier when I couldn't stand you. Now, I can't even read you half the time. I can't even read *me*. I don't know how to be your friend, but I want to try. I mean, we work together, for Christ's sake."

"I'd like to be your friend too." But I don't want to be her friend. Not just her friend, that is, but I can get over that. I can get past that with time. "Like you said, we work together. Maya was getting on me about putting the moves on you and jeopardizing that. All I want is to help you guys out with the work you're doing, because I really believe in it, and I really believe in you."

Maybe that was a little too far, but there's no way to shove the words back in once they've been said. I mean, Sterling is a huge company, and the charitable donations and medical advancements alone are incredible. And Livvy? Olivia is a powerhouse. She does everything she can to devote herself to her work and cares so much about everyone impacted by Sterling Innovations. Everything she does is with consideration to others, whether it's environmental impact, employee advocacy, consumer affordability... the list goes on and on. She won that award and scored her TED Talk because she's not just great at her job, she's the best.

That's not to say Dom isn't also incredible. He's a genius, and even with his hard exterior, he's a softie at heart. The two of them are making changes in the world that I knew I had to be part of, and now that my impact is essential, I don't want to give up.

I'm so proud of both of them. I want to look out for both of them.

I may not have been able to keep every promise I made to her, but I did swear that I would do whatever I could to protect her, to back her up, and even though she'd probably rather I keep my distance, I don't intend to go back on my word.

"You believe in me?" she says. She smiles, genuinely, and as it splits across her face, bathing me in warmth, I decide that there's nothing I'd rather do for the rest of my life than see her smile like that again. I swear, her eyes hold the sun in them.

"Of course I do."

The fact I believe so much in her is why I left her in the first place. I was only going to hold her back, and she's a supernova, she deserves to burn bright all on her own, and the last thing she needs is anything tying her down. She belongs in the sky, she deserves a canvas to paint.

"Am I still invited to San Diego?" I ask.

She snorts. At the sound, she covers her mouth and laughs harder. "Oh my God, that was so unattractive."

I thought it was adorable, but I know better than to say as much. She's laughed the same way since we were kids, with that same scrunch of her face, the same snort, the same smile that splits open her entire face and shows off all of her teeth. It's an infectious laugh, and I'm relieved to see her brightening again.

After knowing what her face looked like when I broke her heart, that crumple as tears poured from her, I'd give anything to see a hundred more of those smiles and hear a hundred more of those laughs.

"Yeah, you can still come to San Diego," she says. "I need the date. It's such a stupid optics thing, but I've heard again and again how important it is for me to be successful *and* attached and strutting around with man candy. I know I probably should've found a guy the organic way, but the auction seemed easier and Dom sold me on the idea. So, if you wouldn't mind doing me the favor…"

"Well, charity calls," I say. "Besides, it's your night to shine and show off. Someone has to take photos for Dom and your mom's Facebook page."

"You're friends with my mom on Facebook?"

"Your dad too. The two of them are obsessed with posting the most random stuff. They added me as soon as they made their profiles."

My mom is even worse. I guess it's nice to know what my mother gets up to over the course of her day, because she keeps her Facebook profile active like some kind of diary, but I've also given her the ability to tag me in what can only be described as humiliating past photos. She's not the best photographer, and has this ability to capture all of my worst angles for the world to see.

But, it's the only social media profile I've kept. I know Livvy and Dom had it back in the day, but Dom deleted his and Livvy abandoned hers years ago. I think her profile still says she's a student at Yale... not that I spend time checking it out or anything. I will admit the photos of her, the pieces of her life I've seen through her parents, always gave me a small spark of joy. I couldn't be in her life, but I could still cheer her on.

Social media does make me feel like a bit of a creep, though. And Facebook has been overtaken by bored, newly retired parents.

She giggles. "The fact you have a Facebook page... I didn't know anyone still uses it."

"I play a lot of Words With Friends," I admit. "It's a trap. Stay far, far away."

When we're talking like this, it almost feels like old times. Like none of the bad stuff ever happened and adulthood never ruined our friendship. Like we can finally talk again, in that way we've always talked with each other. I always felt like there was no one in the world who got me as well as Olivia, and I've been homesick trying to find anyone else who makes me feel that way. Sure, the Balboa Boys and I are practically brothers, but that connection I have with Livvy has been missing for so long I could almost forget.

Friends. I have to be friends *with her,* I remind myself. It's too easy to forget the lines when I get caught up in her gaze or her easy sense of humor. I swallow hard, pushing my reverie behind me, and remember where we are, what we're doing, and the very real possibility my sister may question what's taking so long.

"We better get back out there before Maya thinks we're hooking up," I say.

"Or that we've killed each other and they're about to discover our corpses," she says.

I head outside first, and a few moments later, she follows behind me. Thankfully, no one questions our return or wonders where we've been. Maya and Dom are busy chatting, our parents are catching up, and as the sun dips down low and scrapes against the ocean, I close my eyes, take a breath, and enjoy this moment for what it is.

For the first time since the surreal blur of joining Sterling Innovations, I'm starting to think I'm exactly where I'm supposed to be.

13

Olivia

You can call me a Scrooge, but I hate holiday parties.

I know the point of the company party is to bond with the employees and make them feel appreciated. I mean, I would've assumed giving them quarterly raises during peak performance months and random Starbucks gift cards would also accomplish that task, but Maya seems convinced that large holiday parties are a requirement for longevity, and once she convinced Dom that his "sheet cake in the break room" hoo-rah wasn't enough, we were forced into an extravaganza I tried to avoid at all costs.

Dom rented out the penthouse and rooftop of a nearby five-star hotel for the occasion. Between the open bar and the champagne flutes being paraded around the room, I'm sure everyone here is on the fast track to being insufferably drunk. At Sterling, in our San Francisco branch, we have five hundred employees. Five. Hundred. Dom and I would never dream of treating our coffee cart attendants as less important than our accountants, but that also means the guest list is very, very full.

I know it's important to mingle with our employees, and it's not that I don't like them, but when you're an introvert, parties like this can be a struggle. I've been clinging to the wall, ignoring anyone who tries to throw a line at me.

The decor is minimalist, but the lights and photo station are a cute touch. Maya's even set up a hashtag and a donation station for a few charities Sterling sponsors during the holiday season. Every holiday is represented in some capacity, though I know most of our company is pretty secular. Regardless, the party looks great. There are a ton of snacks and holiday treats, and a live band is playing holiday hits in the corner.

I've been glancing at my watch, wondering when the most socially acceptable time to dismiss myself and make a quick escape is. I can't leave too early and risk being rude, and I don't want to stay too late and completely drain my social battery.

This is the perfect way to ring in the weekend (not).

"You look miserable, Liv," Maya says, hooking her arm through mine and dragging me around the room to make laps with her. "Cheer up. Quit looking so constipated."

"I do not look—"

"Ah, Miss Hernandez!" Some guy I don't recognize with an orangey tan leans in to give Maya a hug, and she releases me for all of a moment. When her eyes flit in my direction, spelling out a clear *ugh*, I begin to think of polite ways to end this interaction before it reaches new levels of discomfort.

"Oscar!" she gushes. "It's been such a long time."

"Since college," he confirms. "I didn't know you work for Sterling."

"Oh, well, you know. It's a relatively new thing." It is,

and honestly, it's hard to believe she hasn't been a permanent fixture for very long. Maya makes the company better, and everything she touches turns to gold beneath her fingertips. She and her brother have that in common.

I know she probably doesn't want to disclose that she and Dominic Sterling are also an item, because in the same way that I have to put up with the snide comments about how I got my job and nepotism, the crap she hears is a million times worse.

"Well, I'm impressed," he says. But I can tell he's anything but.

"Thanks." She grips the stem of her glass a little tighter, glancing at me. "We better—"

"And who is this?" Oscar asks. He smiles a little too big, and I'm not sure what about it has me so unsettled, but I'm desperate for an out to this conversation. "I don't think we've met. I'm Oscar Smith. I work upstairs in operations as a supervisor. You could say I'm, uh, kind of a big deal."

He's got lifts in his shoes, a desperate need to prove himself, and he's currently looking at me like he thinks he's got a 50/50 shot of getting me into bed. Gross. He's clearly overcompensating for a number of things, the least of which being his obvious Napoleon complex, and the whole thing is hard to witness.

Maya looks like she's struggling not to laugh. I take a moment, wondering if he's figured out who I am yet. When there's no recognition in his eyes, I decide to introduce myself properly. If he's not a massive idiot, maybe he'll see his own way out.

"Olivia Sterling," I say. "CFO. You could say *I'm* kind of a big deal."

He blanches for all of a moment before narrowly recovering. "Sorry, Miss Sterling. Didn't recognize you."

"Happens to everyone," I reply. "If you'll excuse us, Mr. Smith."

As I pull Maya away from him, we only get a few feet away before she bursts into laughter, stifling her amusement in her hands.

"Oh my god!" she exclaims. "He's kind of a big deal, Liv. Did you know?"

"Thank goodness he informed me," I deadpan.

She snorts. "I can't believe he tried to hit on you. I mean, I can, but wow. What an ass."

"How do you know him?"

"UCLA," she says. "He ended up transferring after a semester because Mommy and Daddy couldn't buy him a decent GPA. He was definitely bribed in. Don't worry, he was just as charming then as he is now."

"Good riddance," I mutter.

Maya heads back to Dom's side, and he immediately lights up the second she tucks herself under his arm. She has that effect on him, which is strange, given the fact my brother has never been particularly big on smiling. When she drags him over to me, he immediately shoots me a sympathetic look.

"Is it time for a code word?" he mutters.

When we were kids and needed to leave somewhere quickly, we'd signal to each other by using the word 'octopus' in casual conversation. I know that's what he means, even though I'm pretty sure there's no point in using it.

We're stuck. For now. A lot of my favorite employees from communications couldn't make it out, and I've always liked the IT guys, who celebrate women in STEM routinely and always have nice things to say, but it seems all of the friendly faces are elsewhere at the moment. I'm doing my best to keep my head on straight, but my anxiety is twisting my heart in my chest.

Gia finds me next, thankfully with an extra glass of champagne in her hand. When she passes it to me, I'm relieved. "Thank you, G."

"Anytime," she replies. "You looked miserable."

"No one has the holiday spirit," Maya says, faking a pout. "You, Dom... Geez."

"I'm not a party person," I admit. "How have you been, G? You've missed a few girls' nights."

"Oh, you know, Mom's latest boyfriend sucks and she wants to whine about it. My landlord busted another pipe doing DIY construction to save money. A guy peed on my shoe when I rode the BART to a dancing night at the club. But, I read a fantastic book and recently and did some sketches for the office redesign."

"I wasn't aware we were *doing* an office redesign," I reply.

"If you decide you want a cool new office and a set-up for your favorite assistant slash bestie slash fashion consultant, it's all mapped out!" she exclaims. "I mostly just did it because I was bored the other day."

Gia is so creative sometimes that it blows me away. I've wanted to get her into her own office a number of times, but no matter how many times Dom and I ask, she holds strong. I love seeing her ideas when she shares them, though, and she's one of my favorite people to talk to. Her life updates are sometimes so chaotic, but she breezes through them like they're nothing more than an abstract piece of gossip. I've tried to press her for more details, but she doesn't like to complain.

"We should get together this week!" Maya gushes. "Just us three. We could do Christmas manicures. Tis the season, right?"

"I can make it work," I say. "But I've been—"

"Really busy," Gia says in unison with me. "I've tried to

get her to go out with me a million times. It's like pulling teeth."

"Glad to know it's not just me," Maya replies.

"You guys just like the club scene more than I do," I reply sheepishly. "And besides, my Tequila tolerance is rough. Whenever I try to drink at your pace, I end up on the bathroom floor well before last call."

"So the salon is perfect then," Gia says, squeezing my hand. "Maybe we can play bingo after, since you're an old lady."

I shoot her a look, my mouth pressed into a line. We keep talking, the conversations swelling around me. The holiday music and twinkling lights are atmospheric and fun, but I'm not feeling super great, and the room seems to fall away in a dizzy blur.

Dom glances at me, frowning. "Are you okay? You're looking a little pale, sis."

I blink, nodding. "Yeah. Totally."

I figured the lightheadedness was due to the champagne in my system, but when I feel my phone buzzing with an alert from my CGM, I realize it's a matter of not keeping up with my sugar. Dammit.

I don't want to sit down and deal with the attention hypoglycemia brings in a room full of strangers, and after the month I've had, trying to prove myself to everyone, the last thing I need is to show the chink in my armor, revealing all of my weaknesses to a bunch of people who don't deserve to know me that intimately. Business is swimming in a shark tank, and the last thing I need to do is put my blood in the water as bait.

I politely excuse myself, clutching my bag a little tighter as I head to the coat closet. It's currently unattended, so I don't have to worry about explaining myself as I slip inside, sit down, and dig through my purse for my M&Ms.

I know dinner *after* the party was a bad plan. I figured I could reward myself for socializing with a pizza and Netflix on the couch, but I should've eaten something before this moment. The dizziness will pass—it always does—but I find myself frustrated. I'm supposed to be more on top of my diabetes, especially with my new monitor put in, but for whatever reason, I've failed colossally at it.

When the door opens, I scramble, trying to find a place to hide and realizing there isn't one. Thankfully, or maybe unluckily, it's only Alex. He's looking particularly handsome in his tux, and even though his hair is wilder than usual, he's as sharp as ever. All of us are well-dressed, but he puts my red dress to shame with his effortless handsomeness.

"You got a coat tag?" I ask.

He shakes his head. "Wasn't aware you were working a side hustle tonight."

"Oh, you know, money is tight these days."

"Are you okay?" he asks. "I saw you rushing out of the party. Wanted to make sure you weren't passed out somewhere."

"Rest assured, I'm very alert. Well, mostly." I eat another handful of candy, shifting uncomfortably on the folding chair I found stuffed in the corner. "I'll be back out soon. No need to babysit."

"You should probably eat more than just some candy," he says. "I mean, didn't you have a salad for lunch? And I'd be willing to bet you skipped out on breakfast. There's only so much snacks can do to hold you over."

"I'm fine, *dad*." I finish off the M&Ms. "Are we done here?"

He shakes his head. Surprisingly, his voice is firm, a lot firmer than I expected. He's still gentle, not being forceful, but I know he won't let this go. I can't decide how to feel about it.

"Not until I know you're okay," he murmurs. "I saw you looking at that app on your phone - what are your blood sugar levels?"

I cross my legs, curling away from him. "Does it matter?"

"I know it takes a minute to go back up, but I can't do much without a baseline amount. Where are you at?" he asks again. "Please, Livvy. Work with me here."

Reluctantly, I rattle off my numbers. I look down at my phone, taking the numbers in. He sighs, and clearly it's not what he wanted to hear.

"Let's go," he says.

"Go where?"

"To get you some real food. My favorite Thai place is right around the corner and I know you love Pad See Ew just as much as I do. Let me buy you something to eat so I don't have to worry about you turning into a fainting damsel in the middle of the holiday gathering."

Thai is my favorite. Obviously, Dom knows that, but I'm surprised Alex remembers.

I half-wonder if getting Thai food alone counts as a date. It feels official enough to count, even if it wasn't planned. A small part of me doesn't want to ask, though. For some reason, I don't want to miss out on more chances to see him. I want as many as I can get.

"A damsel, huh?"

He shrugs. "You're telling me you don't want to leave? Have you suddenly become a party person? You didn't seem like a party animal tonight."

The thought of him checking me out, his eyes on me throughout the party, turns my blood molten. Warmth blooms through me. "You were watching me?" I ask.

"I'm always watching you." He pauses, then laughs uncomfortably and rubs the back of his neck. "That came out wrong. I just meant that I pay attention to you. I notice you. I can't help it. I've always looked out for you, and I don't know if I'll ever stop."

I know he and Dom had a pact when I was younger to protect me, probably born out of an obsession with *The Princess Bride* and all the other movies little girls worship, dreaming of a prince with an unyielding sense of chivalry, the kind of person who stays loyal to her and defends her honor. I've never considered my honor being in question— I mean it's not 1500—but they were always there when my sugar was low or a girl was mean on the playground.

He offers me his hand. "So what do you say? Dinner?"

I nod, and with hesitation I can't quite place, I take his hand.

I almost expect him to let go when I'm on my feet, but he doesn't. I don't know how we got to the point of holding hands, and I know I shouldn't be spotted walking around with our fingers interlaced like we're some kind of couple, but I can't bring myself to care.

Maybe it's the champagne, maybe it's the fact it's Christmastime and I've always been a closet romantic. Regardless, I let Alex hold my hand in his, strong and warm, and he leads me a few blocks over from the hotel.

A lot of the restaurants in the city are squished between buildings. Some of them are so small there's hardly any space for customers to sit, but the way I figure it, the closer we are to the kitchen, the more we can enjoy the smells wafting out of it until the food arrives.

Alex seems to have my order down to a science, and I'm glad I don't have to tell him what I'm hungry for. As we sit down in the corner of the restaurant with bowls to dig into, I catch myself sneaking glances at him. What girl wouldn't be thrilled about a guy buying her Thai food and rescuing her from a miserable party? I shouldn't be overthinking it.

But I am.

Ever since we talked at family dinner, things have been tense. Almost like we're skirting around something big, but refusing to admit it. I don't know how to place the feeling, but I'm pretty sure it's more than friends territory.

He's an attractive guy. This is normal. Nothing more than basic attraction.

Aside from my vibrator, it's been a while since I've had any action. I'm sure it's normal that I'd be fixated on a handsome man who's just my type. That's normal, and it would usually be something I could write off, but the more I look at him, the less I see myself writing it off. I'm far too attracted to him for my own good.

How much longer can I resist?

"So are you thinking you wanna fly to SD or drive?" he asks. "I know Dom has a jet. Hell, so do I. Well, Miles and I."

Of course he has a private jet. I'm not surprised, though knowing him, he probably doesn't use it too much. He's always been an environmental type.

"I hate flying," I say. "I was going to drive."

"Ten hours?" he asks, brows raised.

"It wouldn't be the first time." I know how inconvenient it is to drive everywhere, but I've always preferred it, and after a certain point, you get used to it. I figured we wouldn't necessarily travel together, but I get the impression that isn't an option.

"I can't believe you're still afraid of flying," he remarks. Even when we were kids, I was terrified of heights. Some things never change. He and the other Balboa Boys are cliff-divers and sky-divers. Me? Not so much.

"I did plenty of it going back and forth from Yale. Believe me, I'm good."

He smiles. "Guess we're driving."

We. I like the sound of that.

14

Alex

Livvy smiles at me across the tiny restaurant table and I'm a goner.

I was checking her out during the party. How could I not sneak looks at her? She has so much power, such a commanding presence that the whole room has no choice but to pay attention. She's a force to be reckoned with. Always has been.

"Are you feeling better?" I ask. "I can get you another soda."

She shakes her head. "I may have low blood sugar, but I still have a tiny bladder."

"We can take as many bathroom breaks as we need."

She rolls her eyes. "You haven't changed a bit. You used to get me so many refills when we went out that I was always rushing off to the bathroom in the middle of our date." It was a running joke that Livvy had TWB (teeny-weeny bladder), and it's nice to see that it hasn't changed. The fact she can be so consistent, like an anchor in a storm, makes me happy in ways I can't quite put to words.

"My sugar is fine," she says at last. "Thanks for rescuing me."

"You're welcome. I needed to get out of there anyway. One of the office clerks was trying to trap me under some mistletoe. How did *that* make it through HR?" It was an attempt I evaded expertly, although there had to be money bet on it or something, given how persistent her attempts were. I'm sure my sister thought it would be cute for photo ops or something, but it ended up just being an annoyance.

"This asshole tried to hit on me by telling me what a 'big deal' he is," she retorted. "It was so ridiculous. You should've seen his face when I introduced myself."

"Good riddance to him," I say with a laugh. "He should know better than to underestimate you."

"They never do," she replies.

I change the subject. "So about San Diego..."

"Yeah?" she asks.

"I called the hotel you're staying at to book a separate room, and they told me they were all reserved for the conference and awards ceremony. Fully booked out all weekend. I figure I'll have to stay a few blocks down or something, but I'm worried I'm going to run into the same problem."

I wasn't originally going to say anything, but I know Olivia is Type-A and will be stressed enough that weekend. I don't want to give her anything else to worry about, so I figure a heads-up will avoid unnecessary confusion and make it easier for her to breathe. I didn't want to assume we'd share a room or anything, especially since this is supposed to be our final date and nothing more, so I'm surprised when she almost seems... happy with the hotel situation. She tries to mask it by slurping more of her soda, but I catch the flicker of hope before she replies.

"You can stay with me," she says. "I mean, I'm sure there's a pullout couch or something."

"Yeah," I say. "That's fine. Great actually."

"Totally."

She wets her bottom lip, curling it between her teeth, and my eyes fall to her full, perfect mouth. I almost wish we had some mistletoe of our own at this moment, so I could find an excuse to kiss the hell out of her. All night, I've been drugged by her perfume, chasing the high of being around her until I'm reminded that we aren't together and I'm only kidding myself with daydreams.

After we finish eating and clear off our table, we step out into the chilly night air. She shivers, and before I can think twice about it, I throw my suit jacket over her shoulders, bundling her in it. She sighs in relief.

"Did you park in the garage by the hotel?" I ask. "If not, I'll walk you to your car."

"Oh shit!" she exclaims. "I rode with Maya after work today. She's my ride. I should probably go track her down—"

"I can take you home," I offer. "It's no problem."

Her eyes meet mine, and she smiles. "You sure?"

"Positive." There's nothing I'd rather be doing. Nothing at all. Plus, I have no idea if Maya and Dom are off somewhere making out, and that's a thought I don't particularly want to entertain. Selfishly, I want more time with Livvy.

"Hey, Alex?" she says.

"Yeah?"

I'm not sure what I'm expecting her to ask. She seems a little hesitant, like she's on the verge of talking herself out of it, but she clearly thinks better of it because she forms the words.

"When was the last time you... had a date?" she wonders.

"With you. At the shelter?" I thought that was kind of obvious. We're both workaholics. It's not the kind of thing that yields a lot of spare time to go around dating whoever the way most young professionals in the city might.

"Not that kind of date. I meant…" She trails off, considering it. "I mean a date that went *really* well."

Is she speaking in code or something? "I mean, I thought our date went well."

She blushes. "Alex, I'm asking you when the last time you got laid was."

That sends a jolt of electricity straight to my dick, and suddenly I'm rocking a semi without even being touched. I'm a man, after all, and an incredibly gorgeous woman just initiated a conversation about sex with me. Of course I'm hard.

"It's been a while," I sheepishly admit. "I've never been very good at one night stands, even though Miles seems to think I should just get over myself and have one whenever the urge strikes. I've just never been as good at it as he is."

We both laugh a little at that. As we step into the parking garage and make our way towards my car, I try to think un-sexy thoughts to calm my dick down. So far, it's not working. Any glimpse of Liv in that dress and I'm hard again.

"Why do you ask?" I arch a brow, holding open the passenger door for her.

She flushes a little redder. "I guess it was just on my mind."

"Oh yeah?"

"Well, we're friends, aren't we?" she asks.

I've been avoiding using the F word, just in case she decided it was absolutely unacceptable, but now that she's the one floating it, I'm less afraid to nod. I find my voice somehow. "Yeah."

"And we're both unattached professionals with needs," she continues.

"Yeah."

God, I'm a broken record. I feel like a doll with programmed responses, like you could just pull my string to get me to speak one of my signature phrases. In most situations, I'd consider myself to be a smart guy, but when I'm looking at her, thinking about her, my mind is blank.

"It'll probably be better for our working relationship to relieve the tension between us," she says. "I mean, there are all kinds of studies to support that conclusion. Right? It's science at this point."

Is she saying what I think she's saying? Fuck. Yes.

"Exactly." My voice is thick, raspy.

"So…" When her words fail her, when she can't think of anything more, her eyes meet mine, and in the dim light of the car with less than a foot of space between us, I can't fight the heat, the magnetism that draws me to her whenever she's close to me. I'm a moth to her flame, and as I drown in the emerald of her eyes, shocked at how bright they are even in the shadows of the parking garage, I don't pretend anymore. I don't deny my desires.

She sets me ablaze. I take her face in my hands, swirling my thumbs over her sharp cheekbones. I push strands of her hair back with my other fingers, reveling in the feeling of her warm skin. The smell of my cologne on her borrowed jacket collides with her perfume and jasmine shampoo and something else that's just pure Livvy, and I'm desperate to be closer to her.

I don't know who kisses who. I'm halfway into asking the question, or so I think, when she closes the gap, and there's a moment of hesitation that lasts for only fractions of a second before we're kissing frantically, desperately, trying to make up for a decade of lost time.

Her mouth curves into mine, and kissing her unlocks a muscle memory I didn't know I had as her lips mold perfectly to mine, spreading a warmth through me that sets every inch of me on fire. I kiss her harder, and she gasps, allowing me to slip my tongue inside of her mouth and taste her. She moans, and the sound is so erotic my cock becomes stone, and she's so close and too far all at once.

I start to guide her up, and she swings her legs over the center console and guides herself into my lap. As her skirt bunches up around her hips, her lacy underwear brushing against the zipper of my slacks, I shiver. God, I only meant to kiss her, but now that I can feel the heat of her, I don't want to stop. The more of her body I feel, the more I want of her. My hands grip her thighs, and as she grinds forward over the length of my cock, I'm an aching mess.

One of my hands slides between her legs, and I cup her pussy under the fabric of her dress, slowly brushing my thumb over her clit. She gasps, and I chuckle and whisper, "Is this okay?" against her mouth. She nods, grinding her hips in affirmation against my palm, and I take the invitation to push her panties aside, her desire slick against the fabric. A finger slides against her slit, teasing her, and when she moans, I gently ease inside of her, watching her face as she opens up to me, begging for more, before I bury myself knuckle-deep in her cunt.

She groans. "Oh, Alex…"

I remember the first time I fingered her. It felt a lot like this, in the cramped space of my first car after the homecoming game. I'd put my hand clumsily down the front of her denim shorts, and she guided me to the most sensitive parts of her, talking me through making her come until she did.

She holds my wrist, applying pressure as she rides my hand. She's so wet that I can feel it all around me, and when I add a second finger, she's all too ready to take me. She's such a petite woman, but she takes my fingers so well.

"There's a good girl," I moan against her mouth. "You like that, baby? You like the way I fuck you with my fingers? Yeah?"

"Yeah," she moans. "Oh, Alex…"

I let her finish once. As I pump my fingers in and out of her sweet little pussy, I watch her face as her eyes roll back, her body tightens and uncoils like a spring, and when she pours herself all over my hand, squeezing me as she rides herself through the finish line, I almost come in my pants. It's so erotic listening to her as she gives into her pleasure, unafraid to show me how I'm making her feel.

I keep touching her even as her aftershocks subside, mesmerized by the way her body responds to me.

Just before she comes again, I stop, pulling my hand back. She frowns in confusion, tilting her head to the side.

"I want to feel you come again," I murmur. "Your place or mine?"

"I'm close," she whispers.

"Yeah," I say, kissing her once more. "You are."

15

Olivia

I know in many ways, I'm one of the lucky girls.

I got to learn sex, or at least parts of it, with a good guy who made me feel safe, loved. Cherished. Alex never made me feel awkward, and since it was a first for him too, we taught each other and explored one another. I have good memories of the way he made me come when we were younger, but when he touches me as an adult, with all the rugged, self-assuredness of a man, I realize he's aged like fine wine in more ways than one.

Holy shit.

I wasn't expecting him to edge me or praise me, but in doing both, he's unlocked kinks I'd forgotten about amid the casual flings. I'm a powerful woman, and I know that, but there's something about servitude in the bedroom that turns me on a hell of a lot too. The only time I want to be led, or told to be quiet, or instructed on what to do, is when I'm in the bedroom.

Alex looks like he knows how to dominate a woman, how to experience pleasure wholly and completely. You don't get to a financial status like his by being uncertain, and he's too confident for me to believe he's hesitant in the sack.

As we drive to my place, the radio humming softly in the background, my heart beats with anticipation. I'm nervous, but it's not a bad thing. The excitement and anticipation of what comes after an amazing orgasm has my toes curling. If he could make me see stars in his cramped car, surely what follows is going to be even more amazing.

We head upstairs, and as the elevator climbs to my floor, he glances over at me. "You okay?"

"I'm great," I say. My cheeks are red, my fingers are clutching my purse tightly, and I find myself torn between which part of him to undress first, all the places I want to kiss. I knew his body well years ago, but now there are new rigid lines of muscle to explore, new parts of him to taste.

"We don't have to do anything," he murmurs, as we reach my front door. "I can leave it at this, say goodnight."

"I don't want to," I say softly. "I want…"

He breathes a sigh of relief. "Me too."

I almost expect a frenzied, hot kiss when the door opens, but he surprises me. Gently, he pushes me against it and locks it behind us, his knee between my thighs, his hands on my waist. He kisses me like he's memorizing the shape and dimensions of my mouth, like he's learning everything he can about me.

His lips are soft sliding against mine. The roughness of his stubble is the perfect contrast to his mouth and those full, gorgeous lips of his. He takes his time kissing me, stealing my breath away and giving me his in hot, raspy gasps. When he nibbles my lower lip and sucks it between his teeth, I groan embarrassingly loud. He has a way of bringing sounds out of me that I didn't know I was capable of making, and it's sexy as hell. The moan allows him to slide his tongue into my mouth, and I can't fight the next one that bubbles out of my throat. I claw his back through his shirt, and he lifts me into his arms, pinning me fully against the front door, my body flush with his and the wood.

He grabs my ass, squeezing and pushing me so that my hips are aligned with his. I can feel his cock hardening under the zipper of his slacks. Even at partial mast, it's fucking huge. I'm surprised by it, even though I've seen him naked before. It feels like discovering something new, completely uncharted territory from here on out. I feel like my body's missed him somehow, like it's attuned to his in a way it's never been with anyone else.

Is it possible? To remember lovers like they leave impressions?

His hands leave my ass and travel up my bare back through the flowy fabric of my dress, then come around to cup my breasts through the lace of my bra. His thumbs are at the edge of my nipples, avoiding the peaks as though he's intentionally trying to torture me. They pebble anyway. Even my breasts are begging for his attention, begging for him to touch me.

Holy fuck, what is he doing to me?

When he finally strokes my nipples through the thin cups of my bra, I have to do everything I can to keep myself from whimpering. As he kisses my neck, I cover my mouth with my hand, surrendering to his pleasure. The relief of his touch makes me feel like I'm being tortured. I want more. I want to feel him. If I have to wait any longer, I'm sure the excitement might kill me.

"You like how I touch you, sweetheart?"

I nod. *Sweetheart.*

"Use your words, baby," he orders. He's so commanding, and the way it rolls off his tongue, all lust and longing, all but undoes me in an instant.

"Yes," I whimper.

"Open your mouth for me."

His thumb swipes along my lower lip, and I let him in without hesitance. He pushes his finger into my mouth, and I suck obediently, staring into his molten chocolate eyes and watching him react. I imagine it's his thick, veiny cock I'm choking on, taking his finger as deep into my mouth as I can, sucking in a way I know is driving him wild. His dick twitches against my pussy, and even through the layers of clothes, I can feel how turned on he is. I wonder if he knows that I'm dripping against my panties. I haven't stopped. I've been craving him, missing him, since his fingers left my pussy.

Finally, he carries me to the couch. I know he hasn't seen my apartment well enough to navigate past this room, and I'm so desperate for him that I'd fuck him on the floor if it meant feeling his cock sooner.

He sits down in front of me, running his fingers along the zipper on the side of my dress. "Take this off for me, Livvy."

I draw the zipper down, expecting him to assist me, but he doesn't. He just watches me do it, hungrily eyeing my bare legs as they hit the floor.

"That's a good girl. Unclasp your bra for me."

I unclasp it slowly, and when that fabric pools on the floor, he takes in the sight of my bare tits, my cherry nipples standing on end for him, and admires me as if I'm a painting, taking in every curve like it's a brush stroke at a museum.

"You're so fucking beautiful, Olivia," he says. He doesn't use the word lightly, like he's throwing it out there just to get me naked. He says it with reverence, with the sincerity of a man who has nothing to lose or gain, who just says what he's thinking because he *can.*

"Your turn," I say. I don't trust myself to say anything

else, anything that won't give away the storm of confusing emotions swirling around in my mind. All I know is what I want, how badly I want it. I feel like I've spent a hundred years without water, and I'm finally faced with a drop to drink.

He undresses quickly, shedding layers with deft precision until he's almost completely naked. When he's down to his boxer-briefs, I admire the lines of muscle on his body, the light trail of hair beginning below his bellybutton and disappearing into his underwear. Pointing the way to where I want to be as soon as humanly possible. I want to lick every ridge of his abs, when I can take my time. If I counted them, I'm pretty sure he'd have an 8-pack. He never used to be this muscular, but he's grown into his frame. He lets me relish in the sight of his body before he sits down beside me on the couch, spreading my legs.

"Lie down on the sofa," he says. "And spread those pretty legs for me."

I'm all too happy to oblige. I don't know what he's going to do next, but I don't care as long as I get some relief for the need building inside of me. I didn't know I could want someone this much, crave a man so desperately, but Alex is bringing that out in me.

He uses my clothes, the remaining undergarments, to build friction. He sucks my nipples, teasing them and encircling them with his tongue, his fingers traveling down my stomach until they pass the band of my underwear. He gently runs his fingers along my cunt, lighting brushing my clit under the fabric as he moves to suck my other nipple. I remember how tight the car was, how good it felt to take his hand. With the space, he relishes every moment, not rushing.

Fuck, it feels so good. My head spins as he sucks and teases me. He doesn't touch me too much yet, like he wants to take in how wet my pussy is first. When he removes his hand, sucking my desire off his fingers, he kisses each of my breasts.

"You have such pretty fucking tits," he says.

He moves lower. When I expect him to peel away the fabric of my panties, he just pushes them aside. The first lick is across the entrance of my pussy, gathering the moisture on his tongue. He buries himself between my legs, inhaling me.

"Mmmmm," he murmurs. "You taste so good, baby."

I pull on the strands of his dark curls, urging him to keep fucking me with his mouth. I'm already close to another orgasm, and God, do I want to come again for him, hear his encouragement as he drowns in my pleasure as if it's his own.

"No, not like this," he says. Before I can ask what he means, he lays back on the other side of the couch, picks me up like I weigh nothing at all, and sits me down firmly on his face. He's careful not to jostle the glucose monitor on my abdomen as he positions me exactly how he wants me. I don't even have a second to worry about being self-conscious, because he moans so loudly, gripping my hips and pulling me against him, that I can't feel anything but powerful.

He circles my clit with his tongue, sucking gently on the bundle of nerves in a way that elicits a gasp from me. He chuckles, but instead of pulling back, he dives deeper with his mouth. As I get louder, he does too, groaning between my thighs as if my moans are what fuels him. His tongue pushes inside of my cunt, his nose applying pressure to my clit. He begins to fuck me with his tongue, and when my legs begin to shake, he moves up to my clit and pushes his fingers inside of me. He fucks me with his fingers, letting me rock against his hand and mouth as I get closer and closer to the edge.

All at once I come so hard it makes his face slick, and he laps it up until I stop trembling, my orgasm rocking out of me. I cry out his name, "Alex, oh, Alex—" until I'm a mess and trembling. When he flips me again, climbing on top of me, I kiss him, and taste myself on his tongue.

"I need to be inside of you, Livvy," he says. "Fuck, I need you."

He tugs me forward to the edge of the couch so that my legs are hanging off of it, but he doesn't take off his boxers yet. Instead, he guides my hand to feel him through the fabric, which is tenting with his massive cock aching to break free.

How big is he? Seven, eight inches? How am I going to fit him inside of me?

"Should I get a condom?" he asks.

I shake my head. "I want to feel you. I'm on the pill and I've been tested recently."

"Thank fuck. I have too, and I'm all clear." he says. "Your pussy is gonna feel so good on me. So good. I bet you're as tight as I remember."

I want to feel him raw too. I'm desperate to take all of him.

He lifts one of my legs up, over his shoulder, and with his free hand, starts to rub torturously slow circles over my clit again. After a moment, he pulls his boxers down and kicks them off. Now that his cock is free, he's able to ease slowly inside of me, stretching me out as he takes me inch by inch. When he finally bottoms out, both of us sigh in relief. He's so big, and for a second, there's a lot of pressure, but instead of pain, I'm awash with pleasure.

He starts with slow strokes, moving in and out of me gently. When I urge him onward, breathing his name into his skin as he moves over me, he kisses my ankle and starts to fuck me harder. Skin slaps against skin as he buries himself in me, and my moans become encouragement to take me deeper and harder.

"Fuck, Alex. Yeah, oh god—"

"You feel so good. You have such a tight little pussy," he grunts. "You're so tight, so good for me. That's a good girl. My fucking good girl."

He pauses only to grab my other leg and bring them both over his shoulders. The leverage lets him get deeper inside of me, and I'm already closer to another orgasm. The edge feels dangerously near, and I'm not going to last long with the way he stretches me, spreading me open before him. My tits are bouncing with each thrust, and I'm so aware of the way my body's responding to him. Goosebumps pebble my skin. Every inch of me is at attention, all but begging him for more.

I like when he's rough with me. I like that I can feel his hips slamming into mine, that he stretches me out more than anyone else ever has and that he doesn't let me close my eyes. No, he wants me to look at him while he fucks me, and it's erotic, his heady gaze on mine.

"Eyes on me. Good girl."

I'm a mess of *yes* and *please* and *harder, harder!* The couch creaks against the hardwood floors, but I don't care. I like that our bodies can meet and years of unsaid words and arguments can be poured out into this dance of chemistry.

Alex licks his lips as he drives me deeper into the sofa cushions, which are damp with our sweat and desire. My body is tensing with that unmistakable edge again, the kind that only comes when I'm almost, *almost* there. God, I'm gonna come so hard. I know I will, and as my eyes start to close, he's there, meeting my gaze, coaxing me onward.

"That's my girl. Come for me, baby."

My girl. Something about belonging to him feels a little too good. I know it's not true, and I know I'm not really his, but it's what I need to hear to push me over the edge of oblivion.

I come in a shower of stars behind my closed eyes and sparkling over my skin, like the Fourth of fucking July or something. I never knew coming this hard was possible before this moment, but as everything I'm feeling reaches a crescendo of pleasure, I'm shocked by how incredible I feel. Alex rides it out with me, and when he has an orgasm of his own, he pulls out, spraying cum all over his hand and my belly. The hot semen runs between the valley of my breasts and down my hips, and it feels satisfying knowing I've unraveled him.

Sweat has his wild hair curling and plastered to his forehead. He smiles at me, his gaze sleepy, as though he can't believe what just happened. He leaves me for a second to get a damp rag from the bathroom and returns with washed hands, ready to clean me off.

I'm not sure I can form words yet. As I'm struggling to form a coherent thought, dizzy with the aftershocks of my own desire, he beats me to the punch.

"Wow," he says.

"Wow," I say.

He smiles, dimples indenting his cheeks, and his smile is so familiar I could drown in it. "You sure you want to do that only *once?*"

I smirk. "Well, maybe twice."

16

Alex

Dominic is going to kill me.

When I wake up naked in an unfamiliar bedroom, there's a second that I'm taking in the beautiful Saturday morning, the San Francisco fog out of the penthouse windows and the sun defiantly peeking out of the clouds. It's a beautiful view, a beautiful morning, and after a good night, it's welcome. Then, I remember the night before, realize who the naked woman lying beside me is, and think about the many ways her older brother could butcher me after he finds out. That's the very first thought that crosses my mind when my eyes open. I might have been cool with him and Maya, but Dom is different. He's far more protective over Liv than anyone, and I doubt he'll be keen to give me a second chance with his sister.

What did I just do?

I'd like to regret it, but I don't. The sex was far too amazing to be something I cringe about, and that makes it hard to pretend I didn't enjoy myself. I don't feel remorse for touching her, and I don't regret the many, many orgasms I pulled from her body. To keep my morning wood from becoming even more uncomfortable, I try to remind myself that Dom took a medieval history class and is more than acquainted with creative torture methods. Not to mention, my mother would have plenty of words for me about what a massive idiot I am.

Olivia doesn't stir, and her light snores are so adorable and familiar. When us boys would have sleepovers, she'd sometimes sneak into Dom's bed and crash the party. Even now, she sprawls across the bed, her breath whistling and drool puddling out of the corner of her lips. It's too damn cute.

I slide out of bed, looking for my boxers so I'm not completely indecent, and head out into the kitchen to start making a pot of coffee. If there's anything I know about Olivia, it's that she doesn't play around when it comes to her coffee. I know I don't regret our night together, but things are different in the light of the morning, all cards on the table, no night to hide behind.

The instructions for her damned machine are in Italian of all things, so it takes me a minute to figure out what each of the knobs and fixtures mean. By the time the espresso starts to drip, I hear shuffling behind me. A sleepy Livvy wanders into the kitchen, clad in a large Led Zeppelin shirt and her panties as she rubs her eyes. She normally wears contacts, so seeing her in glasses with her hair pulled into a messy bun is a foreign sight, but a welcome one. Reminds me of simpler times.

I've spent plenty of nights wanting to wake up beside her in the morning. I'm grateful for the chance to have it at least once, to appreciate the sight of her before she puts her face on and gets ready to take on the world. Her softer side is just as beautiful.

"Good morning," I say.

She sniffs, breathing in the smell of the beans. It's a smooth blonde roast, and knowing her, probably imported. She's never been as snobby as Dom with her expensive tastes, but coffee was always an easy splurge.

"You made coffee?" she murmurs. She takes a couple of mugs down from the cabinet. I laugh when mine says *#GIRLBOSS* in pink sparkly lettering on the side. Hers says *World's Best Dad* and definitely came from a thrift store, and it's charming. Completely Olivia.

"Of course, we were up late, and I figure it's probably best to recharge." I wince. Maybe that wasn't the right thing to say. I'm not sure how to skate around the topic of sex, and admittedly, I haven't needed to before this moment. I want to respect her cues and address everything at her pace. Whatever that looks like.

"Yeah," she agrees. "I hope you, uh, slept okay."

As she foams some milk for hers, the room is so silent you could hear a pin drop. Benedict comes tearing around the corner to his automatic feeder, munching happily the second it beeps, and we both stare at him like a damn cat is the most engrossing thing on the planet.

"We should probably talk about last night," she says. "It was…"

Amazing? Mind-blowing? Fantastic sex? "A mistake?" I guess. I don't want to hear her say it never should've happened, but I've been around her long enough to predict what's on her mind. I brace myself for her confirmation, but it doesn't come.

She shakes her head. "No, it wasn't a mistake. I don't regret it, and honestly it was long overdue. Gia is always telling me I need a dick appointment."

"A dick appointment?" I snort. "Really?"

I've heard similar statements from Miles, and while he has creative opinions about what I should do to handle my bachelor status, I haven't heard a term that amusing before. It's certainly a new one. When I raise a brow, her blush deepens.

She laughs. "I know it's a weird way to put it. You don't have to tell me."

"Well, I had a great time," I say. "Nothing wrong with two consenting adults letting off some steam after a high pressure job. Gotta do what you gotta do."

"Right?" she says. "Exactly."

"I do think we should keep it between us. If Maya finds out, it goes to Dom, and if Gia finds out, who knows who she's going to tell about it."

"I get what you mean," she agrees. "Between us, then. It was a one time thing."

"As I recall it was a three time thing," I correct her. And if memory serves, I ate her out between rounds of sex, keeping her sated until she was completely out of energy. It was pretty great. I channeled years of wishes, fantasies while I jerked myself off, into this moment. Odds are, it's the only one I'll get, so I needed to make it count.

She blushes. "Oh, right."

"Do you want it to stay a one time thing?" I ask her slowly.

The erotic images that flood my mind in a supercut reel are enough to make any guy weak. Our sweaty bodies were entangled everywhere, and I'm pretty sure her panties are still wedged somewhere in the living room couch, not to mention all the other bodily fluids that probably can be found with a black light.

If I had it my way, I'd end every day like last night, tangled up in her, claiming her body with mine. I'd breathe her in, taste her, learn every inch of her skin. It's a hell of a way to live, and honestly, the only way I want to live. It's like the first bite of forbidden fruit has revealed that I am starving for her.

She bites her lip. She bites that lip, and I remember what it felt like to have it between my own teeth. "I don't know, to be honest. I thought it would be out of my system, that I could just go back to my life and not think about sex for the longest time, but now that I've done it, and you're here, I'm having trouble forgetting."

Fuck. The implications of her words, however vague they are, make my dick twitch. Does that mean she wants to do it again? That she feels the same pull between us, drawing me into her?

I'm going to become an addict at this rate.

"It could get complicated," she warns me. "I mean, Dom notices everything. Surely he's not gonna turn a blind eye to this…" She gestures between us with her hand, back and forth. "*Situation*."

"Situation, huh?" It feels like we're Bond villains discussing a heist when she puts it that way. "I get what you mean. We never speak of it, and never act on our attraction again. I'd like to keep my nose the way it is."

"After Dom beats you up, he'll be pissed at me for fucking his best friend," she says. "If you go down, we *both* do."

"So on Monday, we pretend it never happened," I confirm. "That's easy enough, yeah?"

"Yeah," she says, but her voice gets a bit higher, squeaking out as if she doesn't quite believe it. "Easy."

I set my mug of steaming coffee down on the counter, stepping a little closer to her. "You know, we've already had sex today. Well, early this morning. And Monday is still almost forty-eight hours away."

She swallows hard.

"What do you say we get the most out of our weekend?"

She sets her mug down on the counter and looks up at me with wide doe eyes. Her hand trails down my chest, stopping at the waistband of my boxers. She bats her eyelashes before her fingers graze my cock through the fabric, and I feel my throat bobbing with tension.

"I think you've never had a better idea in your life," she murmurs.

I close the distance between us in a matter of steps, and when her silhouette becomes flush with mine, my hands trace down to her hip bones, landing on her ass, which I squeeze greedily. Maybe I'm an ass man, or maybe I'm just a Livvy man, and every inch of her is desirable and perfect.

I'm aware of how warm her thighs are, and as her hips slide in alignment with my groin, all the blood rushes from my head to my cock. I'm sure she can feel how hard I am against her belly, and she whimpers with lust.

Her mouth is so full and pink, lips swollen from a night of kissing. She's only a centimeter or two away from me now, and I can see the bloom of blush in her cheeks, the expression in her green eyes, which storm with purpose. When she makes her mind up, there's no hesitation. Her pupils dilate, and she dives headfirst to kiss the hell out of me. My breath is in her mouth, and the heat of her surges through me as our tongues battle for dominance. I can taste the coffee and toothpaste on her, and while the combination would be disgusting on anyone else, when it comes to her, it's incredible. Euphoric.

I pull her closer. Her nipples are hard under her shirt, worn thin and faded from washing, and I can feel the way she holds her breath at the sensation. She inhales sharply, moaning my name so breathlessly it's almost unintelligible, and kisses me harder, more determined in the way our mouths meet. She's so sure of herself, and all of the reservation of a few minutes ago is replaced with an animalistic passion.

Every part of me is touching her, and I'm already rock solid, straining against the fabric of my boxers. I'm certain if I waste another second not being inside of her, I'll explode with need.

My hands slide up, under the back of her shirt, skimming over the curves of her back like waves on the sea. My palms cup her breasts, and my thumbs trace the pebbled skin of her nipples, hardening them into peaks. She shudders against me, moaning as I caress her skin, twirling her nipples beneath my fingers. She braces herself, gripping my wrists to encourage me to keep touching her, rocking into me.

I shift, using her hair to pull her head back, baring her throat to my lips. I kiss down her neck, taking my time to feel her heart race, skipping beats beneath my wandering tongue. I lick, nibble, and kiss all I can of her. Her breathing is shallow, ragged as she reaches her fingers into the hair at the nape of my neck and tugs. I might get a bald spot from the way she pulls, but it's worth it to get this reaction out of her.

I reach down, sliding my hand over the curve of her stomach, careful to avoid her monitor, and revel in the feel of her underwear, lacy and soft as hell. I tease the outside of her panties over her pussy as I work her nipple between my lips, sucking hard until she's strung tight.

Finally, when she can't take the teasing any longer, she pulls my boxers down just enough to free my cock, and I flip her around, baring her ass to me as I push her into the counter. I pull her panties down, and in one fluid motion, sheath myself inside of her, bottoming out as I fuck her deep.

She cries out, gripping the tile. "Fuck, Alex, yeah. Oh, yeah."

She lifts her hips to meet every thrust. Our bodies slam together, over and over again. The tension builds fast. I'm all too aware of how amazing she feels, how slick she is against me. She's not afraid to moan, to be loud enough that I can hear her cry out for me. I grunt into her skin, slapping her ass as I drive her into the counter. It's hot as fuck, being buried inside of her while both of us are partially dressed, as if being apart any longer isn't an option.

"Oh fuck!" she squeaks out. "I'm close. I'm…"

"Come for me, baby," I order her. "I want to feel you come around my cock. Tell me how you like it, tell me how good I fuck you. My good fucking girl."

When she does, it draws an orgasm of my own out of me. I bury myself inside of her one final time, then pull out and spray all over her ass, pouring out every ounce of release until I'm still, breathing hard into her neck, our bodies slick with sweat and pressed together.

She giggles after a moment, and the sound is breathless as it falls from her mouth. "Wow. Who would've thought morning sex could be so…"

"Intense?"

"Oh, yeah," she says, nodding. "I need a shower though."

Benedict hops onto the counter, narrowing his eyes at us. For most of the morning, he was content to mind his own business, but it seems he's ready to let me know I've overstayed my welcome.

"I'm starting to think you might be right," I say with a

chuckle. "Looks like Benedict is judging us for making a mess."

"Well, we can't all groom ourselves."

"But I'll happily help you out," I say, my voice low.

She smiles at me, taking my hand and leading me to the bathroom without another word.

17

Olivia

By the time I finally remember the list of things I need to get done today, I've wasted half of my day in bed with Alex Hernandez making what I can only describe as questionable choices. If it were anyone else, my girlfriends would cheer me on from the sidelines, telling me about how it's time I finally embraced being young and unattached and got dicked down. Because it's my ex? Cue the circus music. Grab me a clown costume.

I don't regret the sex. No, it's too pleasurable and mind-blowing for me to feel regret. The second I come up with a reason why we shouldn't, I can conjure another hundred why we should. The temptation to keep falling into bed with him supersedes any logic.

I like having sex. With my ex. Admitting it to myself elicits a judgment all its own. If I were talking to a friend, I'd be demanding to know what she was thinking or where she envisions it possibly going. Even if the answer is "nowhere, fast" I'd give it a chance to be heard. Everyone needs to be heard.

But, discretion is key here, and I can't talk about this at

girls' night. I'm not just sleeping with my ex-boyfriend and first love, which is messy and complicated for personal reasons, I'm also having sex with my investor and coworker, which is messy and complicated for professional reasons. Even if all the logic in me is screaming, demanding answers, another part of my brain can't be bothered to give a damn.

He kisses my shoulder, startling me out of reverie. "How about we stay in bed all day?"

I wince. "I can't."

"What do you mean you can't? Sure you can."

I shake my head. "I really can't. I need to go shopping and get a dress for the awards ceremony, not to mention more clothes for the rest of the weekend. Between the parties and banquets, I need to be looking my best. There are going to be so many pictures taken, maybe even an interview in *Forbes* and *Time*. These photos have to be perfect. There's no other option."

"Any photo of you is going to be perfect," he says with a groan, like it's obvious. "You've earned this. Take your moment, embrace it. I'm sure whatever you have in your closet is just fine."

"It's not new," I reply. "I talked to Sterling's PR team and they recommended a little extra glam. You know, so I can prove that I *have it all*."

I know optics are part of building a brand and building a brand is part of ensuring a profit, but I feel like I'm being paraded around as some kind of trophy for the marketing team. Dom makes headlines as a handsome billionaire bachelor, and now I'm the designated #GirlBoss proving that feminism is alive and well. Sure, the fact it's so important that I look good definitely feels counterintuitive, but no one asked me for my two cents.

I've been worried about my speech mostly. I want to

say the right things, headline the right magazines, give the right sound bites from my interviews. I almost forgot the fact my clothes, ridiculously enough, have an equal weight in the grand scheme of things. Throughout my younger years, I was an unfortunate victim of my awkward phases, and all of that anxiety that comes with being the girl no one wants to date in college lives in the back of my mind. Even as an adult, there are small cracks in my armor.

Which is why, as Maya is so quick to remind me, I need to make sure I'm suited up in the right kick ass armor: a perfect ball gown. She makes it sound like this occasion is as important as finding a wedding dress and deserves all the same importance, but I know confidence goes a long way. Sure, I navigate the treacherous waters of a male-dominated field all the time, but the competition among women can be equally fierce and bloody.

"It's important for me to be a Renaissance woman. I gotta have—"

"The looks, the brain, and the arm candy." He rolls over with a chuckle. The sheet dips low across his golden abdomen, and he shakes his head. "I'm glad that I get to be a part of it then."

"Arm candy," I scoff. "I never thought a career in medical technology would involve so much primping. I feel like I'm about to debut at the marriage mart."

"Benedict Bridgerton would certainly make for an ideal companion," he remarks. "Look, Livvy, is it possible you're overthinking this? The dress you wore last night is nice."

"And it's currently balled up in a corner somewhere," I point out. Not to mention, my cat probably made a home out of it and got it covered in fur. If it survived last night without any bodily fluids turning it into a Jackson Pollock painting, I'd call that nothing short of a miracle.

"Dry cleaners?" he suggests.

"It's too casual." Which it is, though explaining that to a guy who doesn't care much about fashion is difficult enough.

"I didn't know dresses could be casual. I always figured they were fancy by themselves."

Honestly, he and Dom are too much alike. My brother doesn't know anything about clothes either, despite being well-dressed. When he and Maya started seeing each other, he had the nerve to question why she owned so many pairs of shoes.

Tells you what he knows. I may not be as feminine as Maya or as attuned to trends, but I'm not nearly as helpless as Dom. Honestly, she keeps him sharp and polished, and for that, I'm grateful.

"You're overthinking this," he adds. "You could wear a potato sack and look beautiful. Hell, the magazines would probably think you're making some kind of eco-friendly fashion statement." The smirk that crawls across his face as he stifles a chuckle makes me want to smack him.

I narrow my eyes at him. "Of course this is easy for you to laugh about. You're built like a Greek god and get to just throw on a suit to be GQ handsome. Some of us have to visit the salon twice a month and buy a new closet every season."

"Every season?" he guffaws. "Jesus, woman, and you *don't* want a raise?"

"I don't have expensive tastes," I admit. "But regardless, I have to shop today, and that's why I can't stay in bed having hot, nasty sex with you. As much as I want to stay in bed having sex with you, it's not an option."

"But what I'm hearing is, you want me." He wiggles his eyebrows.

I throw a pillow at him.

"You look beautiful," Alex says, as we're walking toward one of the designer dress boutiques in the heart of the city.

I'm wearing a pair of mom jeans and one of Dom's Berkeley sweatshirts that I stole from his closet years ago. There's nothing particularly extraordinary about my outfit, and I'm not even wearing makeup, but when I catch a glimpse of Alex's face, I realize he's completely serious.

Wow. Okay. I'm not sure what to say about that. I nearly walk into a nearby planter box and narrowly make my recovery, trying to be as nonchalant and unfazed as I can manage. He carries on, and I'm not sure if he noticed my fumble or is just pretending not to have seen it, but either way, I'm grateful.

A bunch of businesses and shopping malls sit next to the Macy's, where the iconic Christmas decorations are up and the ice-skating rink is alive with kids. With the holiday two weeks away, shopping is going to be a nightmare, but I put myself in this position, and now I have to roll with the punches.

Thankfully, the boutique is locally-owned and not nearly as packed as a department store would be.

He reaches for the handle of the door to hold it open for me, and I finally burst open with the whirlwind of emotions that's been brewing under the surface since we got out of bed. All of my inner struggles, doubts, and feelings erupt.

"Would you stop doing that?" I ask.

"Doing what?"

"The charming stuff. It's… a little much, don't you think?" I don't mean for the words to be harsh as they roll off my tongue, but he seems to be a little hurt by them anyway. It's not that I don't want him to spoil me—it's just that I know it's selfish to want girlfriend treatment when we're not anything close.

He blinks a few times in surprise. "Wow. Okay."

"Sorry for being edgy, it's just..." I pause, taking a breath. "If we want to keep our business, you know, our business, then it's probably best we try to keep this as close to our normal relationship as possible. So no compliments, no chivalry. We have to be professionals."

"Professionals who are also going on a date," he says. "Got it."

"And don't be a smart ass. Honestly, take that look off your face."

"What look?" he says. "This one?"

He proceeds to pull a number of faces, contorting his mouth as mockingly as he can. I try to stay annoyed at him, but it's adorable, and something about the way we play around with each other is a little too nice for my taste. If I'm not careful, attraction will become a crush, and a crush will spiral into something far more intense.

As we walk through the aisles of dresses for all sorts of occasions, I start to flick through the rack closest to me, hoping something will stick out. The whole thing feels a little overwhelming between the necklines and fabrics and lengths. I'm so scared of choosing wrong, and no amount of Google searches about previous winners comforted me.

I suck at being a girl.

"What about this one?" he says, holding up a sapphire number that's floor length and strapless. "Blue is definitely your color. It makes your complexion and hair stand out."

I shrug. "I could try it."

"Or this one?" he proposes, holding up an emerald dress with glittery beads and a sweetheart neckline. It reminds me of something straight out of a Disney movie, and I know the color will make my eyes pop.

He holds up a few dress options as we go along, and his opinion is comforting me in the war against my own thoughts. When he pulls a champagne, glittery mermaid dress with a low, sweeping back, I hold my breath. It's stunning, and the fabric ripples as smooth as water. I know it's one of my favorites so far, but we have quite a few by the time we get to the change room.

I don't know why I'm a little disappointed that he doesn't come in with me, but I realize it makes sense that he would wait outside, given my speech about being professional and a bunch of other anxious things I'm not sure I meant.

The gold dress is perfect. It's the first one I try on, and I'm blown away by it. When I step out of the room, nervously shifting on my feet, I watch his eyes follow every curve of my body, taking in every detail of the dress like he's memorizing it for later.

"Wow," he says. "That's amazing."

"I should probably try the other ones on," I say, even though I know I'll be buying this one for some occasion.

"Yeah," he says. "Lots of, uh, events."

Our eyes are locked on each other, and it's like the whole room has melted away and left the two of us to stare at each other, to take each other in.

I shut the door again, appraising the other kinds of dresses I have for each of the events I'm expected to go to. I have a cocktail dress that seems impossibly tight, but highlights my body and pushes my cleavage so high my boobs seem way bigger than they are. It's a little too much skin for my taste, so I decide to throw it back on the rack.

But before I can get it over my head, I realize the zipper must not be down all the way, because I've made myself a prisoner with the dress over my head, pinning my arms towards the sky like I'm some kind of awkward ballerina.

Shit. Shit. Shit!

I struggle, slamming into one of the walls as I try to wiggle my way out of the fabric suffocating me, but it's no use. I'm standing completely exposed with my lacy underwear riding up my ass and no bra, completely exposed for the world to see. Not to mention, if I tear this dress, I'll have to buy it, and explaining the tears to the cashier sounds like a nightmare.

Fuck me. The last thing I want is to ask for help, but I'm out of options.

"Alex!" I finally call out.

"Yeah," he says. "Are you okay?"

"I'm stuck."

"What do you mean you're stuck?"

"In this dress. I'm stuck in the dress."

He pauses. "Come again?"

"I need help getting out of the dress."

He sighs. "Alright."

"But you can't look at me or laugh."

"How am I supposed to help you if I can't see what I'm doing?"

"Figure it out!"

"Okay, okay."

I nudge the door open from my side with my hip, and I hear his heavy footfall as he steps into the room and the lock clicks behind him. For a moment, neither of us says anything, and my face is burning lobster-red. The silence is enough to make me miserable, and I'm pretty sure if the lack of air doesn't kill me, the humiliation of this moment will.

"Say something."

"I'm trying not to laugh," he says with a snort.

Bidding on Love

"And no peeking!"

"Liv, we had sex last night. I've seen you naked. And I'm pretty sure I'm not going to be able to get the zipper undone inside-out without peeking."

He makes a good point, even if I can concede that much. "Fine. Just… don't say anything, okay?"

As he slowly shimmies the dress over my head, I'm relieved and self-conscious and fed up with the excitement of shopping. Getting strangled by a dress wasn't on my Bingo card for this weekend, but at least he was here to help me. I'd have to flash a poor sales associate otherwise, and that would make everything so much worse.

"There," he says, smoothing my hair out of my face. "Crisis averted."

"Right," I whisper.

"I'm going to step out now," he says.

"Yeah, absolutely."

And then I trip, I fall, and the next thing I know, I'm kissing him. I'm kissing him, and he's got me pressed against the wall of the changing room, devouring me with his mouth and reminding, me of all the tricks he can do with his tongue, and I'm whimpering and wishing we'd never left my bedroom.

But before his lips can stray from mine down my neck, an employee knocks and startles me. The poor bored kid must've heard my screaming for help, or worse, thinks we're messing around in here.

Which… we were kind of about to.

"Are you okay in there?" the worker asks.

"Yeah," I say, clearing my throat. "Had a minor fashion mishap, but I'm all good."

"Okay," he says. I'm holding my breath until he leaves, and when he's gone, Alex snorts.

I hold up my finger, feigning authority. "Never again."

"What? The kissing or the dressing room part?" he replies.

"The dressing room," I say, because if we're being honest, I know damn well I can't make any promises about not kissing Alex Hernandez. Even though it defies all good judgment, it's the one thing I'm starting to want more than anything in the world.

18

Alex

I'll be the first to admit that I wasn't expecting Olivia to follow through with our plans to attend the Women in Tech ceremony and conference together.

After the dressing room, the awkwardness, and the tension after a weekend of rough, animalistic sex, I figured she'd either A) ghost me, B) have Gia deliver a message saying my presence will no longer be required, or C) tell Dom what happened, get me fired, and then head to the conference with Dom as her plus one.

None of those things happen. When our travel day rolls around and I arrive at her building to pick her up, she shows up curbside with a suitcase, her dress zipped into a protective bag, and sunglasses on top of her head. Even for California in December, it's pretty sunny. Typical of the city, it's cold and windy, but the sunshine cascades over my windshield and warms my face.

I help her load her bags into the back before returning to my own side of the car. I wanted to get the door for her, but I was already worried I was pushing the chivalry thing too far with helping her grab her stuff, so I thought better of it.

"Hey," she says, climbing into the passenger seat.

Traffic in the city is terrible no matter where you are or what time it is, so I'm already prepared for delays moving forward. The GPS programs our route, revealing the ten hour drive I expected, and I expect her to wince at the ETA, but she doesn't seem fazed.

"You sleep okay?" I ask her.

She shrugs. "I'm kinda nervous. I did my speech four times in the shower, and then I did it again when I was tossing and turning. I've memorized the whole thing, and yet, I'm convinced the second I walk onto that stage, I'm going to forget every single word of it."

"Have more faith in yourself," I say.

"I never feel relaxed until *after* the big speech."

I think few people realize how much stage fright Olivia has. She's always able to overcome it, but in the moments before she gets up there and kicks ass, she almost falters. That's not to say she doesn't have an exceptional recovery every time, but I know how her mind works. I know her better than I know myself, or at least I feel that way from time to time.

I've never liked driving in the city, and least of all, driving out of it and crawling my way out of the Bay Area. The I-5 is full of start and stop traffic, pushing us bumper-to-bumper with plenty of cones, slow-moving roadwork, and good old fashioned rush hour.

You'd think rush hour would be universal, but that's only when you're *not* from California. The fluctuating patterns are anyone's guess these days. You couldn't *pay* me to make this trip on a Friday for anything, but Olivia is my exception to every rule. She doesn't want to fly? Fine, I'll quell my road rage, down a couple coffees, and be her chauffeur.

I haven't taken many roadtrips before—save for the one time Miles took us all to Vegas when Ben, the youngest of us, turned twenty-one. I don't know what kind of things you're supposed to do, and I'm pretty sure Livvy and I are too old for license plate games, so I find myself listening to the radio playing a shuffled mix of all my gym songs, stealing glances at her while she watches the ocean on the side of the bridge out of town.

"We're within walking distance of the beach at our hotel," she tells me, clearly trying to break the silence. "Everything is being held at the convention center, and our hotel is within a mile of a bunch of places to eat, the ocean, and the event."

"Sounds like fun," I say.

"Did you bring a suit?" she asks.

I widen my eyes. "I had to bring a *suit*? Shit, I thought this was a t-shirt and shorts kind of thing!"

Livvy scowls at me, shaking her head. "Okay, Mr. Sarcastic Ass."

"Yes, I brought a suit. Actually, I brought two. And an extra set of cufflinks."

"How many pairs of underwear?" she asks.

I pause. "What? Why?" *Four? Three? Do the ones I'm wearing count? Why is she asking about my underwear?*

"Dom and Maya were arguing about this a few weeks ago. He said you only need one pair of underwear for every day of the trip, and Maya said you need at least three extra pairs."

"And what do you think?" *Oh, shit. Dangerous train of thought. Liv's underwear. Thinking about Liv's underwear leads to thinking about Liv's underwear on her, off of her, in my mouth... Jesus Christ.*

"I think you need plenty of options," she replies. "Period underwear just in case. Comfortable panties if you're not getting laid. Panties people are going to see, panties no one will, thongs for tight bottoms, that kind of thing."

"So how many pairs did you pack?"

"Twelve."

I choke on my breath, laughing. "Twelve? It's a weekend, Olivia."

"Options," she says.

I had no idea underwear was such an important thing to women, but I'm starting to see that now more than ever.

"So the panties you wore to the Christmas party," I start, smirking over at her. "Were those meant to be seen."

"Maybe?" she says. "I wanted pretty underwear in case I found someone to take home."

"You weren't thinking about me specifically?" I know it's stupid to be jealous of a disembodied man who doesn't exist, but jealousy doesn't listen to logic. Now that I've been reminded of her beauty, and specifically, how exquisite it is to get her naked, be inside of her. The thought of any other fucker getting the chance makes me want to rearrange a guy's face.

Her cheeks burn. "Maybe I was."

My cock twitches. "Personally, I had hopes."

"Me too," she says.

"Do you... still?" *Wow. Great line, Alex.*

"Still what?"

"Have hopes of me... seeing your underwear?"

She hides behind her hands, masking the cherry of the blood rushing to her face. "Alex!"

"Well, we are going on a date," I reply. "Sometimes,

dates end with kissing and other things. I'd have to make sure you feel like you're properly celebrating your award. Make you feel special."

She crosses and uncrosses her legs. "Special, huh? And how would you do that?"

I've never been big on talking dirty outside of the bedroom, but she makes me feel brave enough to make more brazen moves. I've spent the whole week thinking about all the new things I'd like to do with her, to her, given the chance. I was masturbating like a teenager all week, all hot for her and high-strung without any idea how to relieve the tension or get it out of my mind.

"I'd start by taking off your panties and eating your pussy in the elevator on the way up to your room. I'd wonder how fast I could make you come, how many times we might almost get caught."

I steal a look at her, trying to pretend the pressure in my boxer briefs isn't about to drive me over the edge. Judging by the looks of her, she's enjoying this just as much as I am. It makes me want her. It makes me feel like I'm not alone in my attraction, like the magnetism between us isn't felt only by me.

She bites her lip. "And then what?"

"I'd kiss you all the way to our room, and then I'd fuck you on every surface in it. I'd make you come over and over and over again until you know how amazing you are, how much you deserve the world. I'd make sure you're properly celebrated, and then I'd draw you a bath, order champagne, and praise you and declare how amazing you are until we're both so exhausted we fall asleep."

I can see it now in my head, feel the way the fabric of her dress would pool around us, imagine the salt of her sweat on the column of her throat. I can imagine the way the bed could rock like a ship on the sea, the way it would feel to hold the headboard and slam it into the wall as I bury myself in her.

"That sounds like it would be pretty incredible," she says. "I might take you up on that."

Fuck. She gave me the go-ahead, and it doesn't matter that we're hours away from the hotel room and the ceremony, because my dick has turned to stone under my zipper, and virtually every reasonable thought has been wiped from my mind like a clean slate.

I take a breath sharply through my teeth. "So are you still nervous about that speech?"

"Not really," she says.

"Good," I murmur.

This trip is going to feel so much longer for a very different reason.

Within sixty seconds (no joke, I counted), the hotel staff unload our bags on the luggage cart, and the valet takes my keys before I have a chance to tell them who we are. Apparently, Liv's guest of honor status speaks for itself. I have more than enough money to get the same treatment, but I've never seen the need for it unless I'm trying to impress a date. I'm a little startled by the whole thing.

"We'll bring these bags up to your room, Ms. Sterling," the bellhop says. "Are you and your boyfriend in the same suite?"

Both of us are surprised by the word "boyfriend" and after exchanging nervous glances, she finally says, "Yeah. Same room."

The hotel lobby, with its crystal chandeliers, endless staff, and well-dressed guests, is packed full of people this evening. I assume most of them are here for the conference and awards ceremony, though the sea of bodies makes it impossible to read any of the signs around the room.

Olivia's face leeches of color as she takes in all of the people. Slowly, she raises her finger, pointing at the portrait of her sitting on a stand at the other side of the lobby next to the bar milling with patrons and two different bartenders mixing cocktails. It's not even that late yet, and the place is packed.

"How long before people recognize me?" she says, swallowing hard. "I look like shit. I've been in the car all day. I didn't know I'd… Do I have to…"

"Hey," I say softly. "Breathe, Livvy. We'll sneak up to our room before no one notices."

"How?" she whispers. "The giant photo doesn't give it away?"

I hand her the hoodie I always keep in my backpack, sliding my sunglasses off the top of my head and putting them on her. "There. Now you're incognito."

She nods her head. "I didn't know there was gonna be this much press *before* the ceremony. I look like a mess."

"You're beautiful," I say. "You always look beautiful."

She smiles, despite her nerves. And in some act of god, she takes my hand.

After we get our keys, and surprisingly make it upstairs without anyone pulling us aside to talk to Olivia, she seems to relax a little bit. I know she's not doubting her right to be here, or her place as an impressive, accomplished woman. I just know she likes to be in control of appearances, prepare herself so she says the right thing. Not that she's ever had any trouble.

I open the door for the room with my keycard, holding it open for her as she walks in behind me slowly. When she flicks the switch on, flooding the suite with light, she starts walking towards the bedroom to unpack her bags. I stay in the living room, poking my head in the bathroom with the heated floors and massive clawfoot bathtub, complete with an additional shower and two sinks. My mind floods with scenarios, my imagination wicked as it considers all of the places I could take her, all the ways I could make her come undone on every surface.

Alex, I chide myself.

"Shit," Livvy says from the bedroom. Even if it's not meant for me, the frustrated tone in her voice grabs my attention right away. At first, I'm worried she forgot something or the staff wrinkled her dress.

"What?" I ask.

"The executive suite is meant for a single VIP guest or a couple," she realizes. "When I called and asked if it could accommodate two people, I was asking if there were two beds or a pull out couch or something."

"Are there not—"

I glance into the bedroom, realizing the massive California King is the only bed to sleep on. The living room doesn't even have a couch, so much as a tiny loveseat, an armchair, and a large desk. The flatscreen and balcony are nice add-ons, sure, but there's absolutely no other option for sleeping.

"Oh," I say.

"I can call the front desk, tell them there's been a mistake—"

"Livvy, you said the whole place was booked. There *aren't* any additional rooms available."

Her lips purse. "I mean, I know we planned for a separate sleeping situation. I'm so sorry, I should've checked. I get that we're... I mean..." She sighs. "If you're not comfortable with it, I can ask them for a cot or something."

"I'm not taking your bed, Liv," I cut her off. "We've

shared before. We can do it again. I'll even cross my heart so you know there won't be any funny business. Totally platonic bedsharing. We can even make a pillow wall in between us."

She laughs. "A pillow wall? We're not nine anymore, Alex."

"Your mother created a truce with pillows as a solution way too many times," I reply. "Can't pretend it hasn't made an impression."

"You know, she told me she was glad you were coming with me."

Those words make me stop for a second. I didn't imagine Livvy would feel the need to share the details of my attendance, but apparently, it came up. "Did she now? How'd she find out?" I ask.

"Dom," she answers. "She asked about the auction, he mentioned I accidentally bid on you, and then I told her you were going as my plus one to keep the asshole reporter guys at bay."

"So she thinks we're friends?" I prod.

"I don't know," she admits. "She winked at me behind Dom's back."

I can't help but chuckle. I think her mom was more upset about the breakup than I was, if that's even possible. We grew up so close that the adjustment to space between our families was a tough, sudden one, but there was never bad blood. I always wondered when she'd tell them her side of the story and all of the friendly pleasantries would come to a crashing halt.

So what does it mean if her mom is *rooting* for us?

19

Olivia

Not to be dramatic, and not to gloriously overstate, but this is the single biggest achievement of my career. I knew that much before this moment, but now that Alex and I are walking through the doors of the convention center, surrounded by people dressed to the nines, it finally snaps into place in my mind.

This. Is. My. Moment.

I was anxious at the hotel at first, sure. I wasn't expecting a giant copy of my professional headshot from the Sterling website to be plastered on display in the lobby. It was a good picture (Miles dated a photographer for about a week), and I didn't *hate* it. I just hated the fact I could be ambushed by people I didn't know, who did know me, when I hadn't prepared any good responses to their questions or even combed my hair after being in a car for almost eleven hours.

This is something I've prepared for, something I dared to daydream about when I was in undergrad and still sleeping with a retainer in my mouth. Before I knew I could actually get here, it was something I contemplated in the shower and wrote into my vision boards.

From the moment Alex and I step inside of the San Diego convention center, arm in arm, I can feel the attention shift to us. It's not just that Alex is handsome, because even between his charcoal suit, his perfectly mussed black hair, and his eyes the color of fine whiskey, they're not all looking at him. They're looking at *me*.

I spent an hour on my hair, curling and twisting and pinning and spraying like I was about to be an extra in a Madonna video. I still don't feel like it's glamorous enough. Like I'm playing dress-up and at any minute, I'm going to trip over my own feet and be a kid in my mom's closet again. In some ways, it's almost like the prom all over again, between his tie matching my dress and the way we're posing for endless photos.

"You're the lady of the hour," Alex says in my ear, brushing some of the hair on my neck aside. "Make sure to smile."

"You know telling a woman to smile is a death wish, right?"

He smirks. "You can punish me for it later."

I can name half the people in my line of sight. They're all famous tech developers, CEOs, economists, Wall Street legends, and a few of them have models and actresses as their dates. It's hard not to feel starstruck when I'm surrounded by a hundred incredible people. Not to mention my fellow nominees, who will all be in attendance as well. When I found out I won, I was shocked. Svetlana Popov was rumored to be on the Nobel committee's watchlist. Hell, I knew some of these people from Ivy League alumni mixers. And somehow, I was here. I'd managed to make the cut, and I'd managed to *win* the Woman of the Year award. Being on the 30-under-30 list is an honor on its own, but making the #1 slot isn't something I could've imagined in my wildest dreams.

Slowly, Alex's arm slides away from mine, his fingers trailing down the length of my arm, brushing my wrist, before our hands fall together. He squeezes my hand reassuringly, and I find myself grounded in his presence, knowing he's just inches away. It's hard not to feel a little out of my depth as a few cameras flash and different executives give me nods of encouragement.

Dom and Maya have both texted me throughout the day to ask how things are going and congratulate me a million times over. Admittedly, I'm not sure this is all real. Am I really here? Doing this?

I know imposter syndrome is normal for everyone, from the people who landed on the moon to artists to women in STEM who are younger than their male peers. Mine is rearing its ugly head now, and I don't think I'll fully process it all until I'm holding the award in my hands and giving my acceptance speech.

Alex and I head to the open bar for a couple of drinks, and admittedly, knocking back a shot helps ease the tension and slow my racing heart. Our seats are in the front row of the main auditorium, which of course, is full of hundreds of people.

The whole event is being live streamed, and I've been reminded by Sterling's PR team, my brother, and Maya, who is trying to launch my social media presence, to make sure my words are ones I like, because they're reflecting on me, the entire company, and probably will be quoted often if I continue my "upward trajectory." These aren't my words, of course, and they definitely don't lighten the pressure.

"Just breathe," Alex tells me. "You already won. Everyone knows exactly why you're here."

He's not wrong; there's a large brochure with the rest of the nominees named on it, highlighting what the award means and our experiences that led to scoring a nomination.

The Woman of the Year Award sponsored by the 30-under-30 Women In Technology committee is a special recognition for a female STEMINIST icon making significant headway in her work, research, and/or inventions. This woman is often accomplished not only professionally, but also philanthropically, and this year's Woman of the Year is no exception...

My bio thankfully covers all of the stuff I struggle to say out loud. It's not that I don't know how to advocate for myself. It's just that naming my achievements makes me feel like one of those asshole men who thinks he's god's gift to women for getting into Yale. It means I get to skip to the good stuff: the part of my speech where I thank all of the incredible people who allowed me to reach this point, tell my story, and encourage people who need it. Bragging about myself sounds more like a nightmare than anything else so I'm glad I can skip that. Sort of.

Olivia Sterling (29, Yale alumn) is the CFO of Sterling Innovations: a medical technology development company based out of San Francisco, CA. She is a graduate of Yale University, summa cum laude, a hall-of-fame speaker for the National Speech and Debate Association, and a recent TED Talk Speaker. Just seven years after Sterling's rebrand and rise to power, Olivia has opened corporate offices in ten additional countries and territories, started initiatives to provide medical equipment to developing countries, and donated 15% annually of her reported salary to a range of charities unaffiliated with Sterling Innovations.

"Wow," Alex says, gesturing to the brochure. "They picked a boring picture of you. You're not even smiling in this one."

"Thanks," I deadpan.

"You're welcome," he says, grinning at me. "You look like one of those attorney billboards. I mean, if you passed the Bar Exam, I'd hire you to my legal team."

"Are you done?" I ask, giggling despite myself.

"Made you laugh, didn't I?" he says triumphantly.

Damn, he's got me there.

As the lights dim, indicating that it's time for everyone to find their seats, I find myself reaching for Alex's hand. I don't know when we developed this habit of holding onto each other, but as my heart beats wildly, he's the only thing I can think of to make the world a bit smaller.

Alex squeezes my hand reassuringly. His fingers are threaded through mine and we fit so well together, like the final piece in a puzzle after a long afternoon of putting it together. His touch is calming, and the way he sweeps his thumb over my knuckles is so familiar that my chest swells with heat.

How have I gone so long without him?

I have to focus. I have to get out of my own head. Oftentimes, we don't have the luxury of pinpointing the biggest moments of our lives, but this time, I do. I do, and I'm in it.

You can do anything, Mom always said. *Dream bigger than you think is possible.*

I'd definitely say this counts as "bigger" than I thought possible.

The whole thing is a surreal blur. Even in the moment, I realize it's going to be the sort of memory I recount in flashes, overwhelmed by the enormity of everything happening tonight. When they finally call my name, and the room explodes with applause so loud it makes my ears ring, I take a second, take it all in, and then I walk onto the stage.

It's not a very long walk. A few yards at most. I focus

on my feet, grateful I wore flats so I wouldn't have to risk falling into Alex's arms the moment I got nervous and forgot how to take steps in high-heels. I almost wish I could bring him up there with me for a steady hand to guide me, but this is my moment, and I know he wants me to have it all to myself.

When I finally reach the microphone, shaking the hand of the presenter who passes me a silver trophy carved into the shape of an atom, the stage lights are so bright it's hard to see all of the faces in the auditorium ahead of me. I get the first row before everyone turns into blobs and shadows, and the one face that feels clear as day is Alex's, and he's smiling and clapping harder than pretty much anyone.

"My name is Olivia Sterling and I'm the CFO of Sterling Innovations," I introduce myself. My voice quavers for only a second, but I clear my throat, regaining my confidence. "I want to thank the committee for voting me for this great honor, but I also want to take this moment to acknowledge the twenty-nine other women nominated for this award tonight. They are all trailblazers, kickass, and making history in this industry. Any one of them would have been more than deserving of this award, too. I'd like to give them a hand."

The room claps again. I steal a precious moment to breathe, grounding myself.

I can do this.

"I'd like to thank my mom and dad first, but I think they should be thanking me, because if I hadn't been born, there would have been no one to keep my insane brother, Dominic in his place." Laughter erupts, and I find myself giggling too. "But I also want to thank him. Dom, you are such an inspiration to me, and you never made me feel like I was living in your shadow. If anything, you reflected light of your own onto me. This is an honor for both of us and the dreams we're creating together. And Mom and Dad, you guys have made all of this possible, too. Thank you for cosigning my student loans so I could go to Yale, and also, thank you, Yale."

I feel like you never realize how many people there are to acknowledge until you're forced to recall them all within the confines of a speech. I'm worried I'm going to miss someone or say the wrong thing, but my mom always says if you speak from the heart, you can't go wrong.

"To all my friends, to all my staff, thank you for supporting me here. This is not a solo effort. This is the result of a team of very talented people who championed me. Without them, I wouldn't be here. Thank you to my grandparents, whose history of chronic illness inspired me to invest in medical technology. I know I shouldn't stay up here forever, so I just want to say this. Once, in my freshman philosophy seminar, my professor said we often have to choose if we want to be loved widely or deeply—"

I pause. Finally, I find Alex again, and his brown eyes hold mine and make everything else fade into the background. Suddenly, we're the only two people in this entire room, maybe even the whole world, and I'm looking at him like he holds the secrets of the entire universe in the palm of his hand.

Of course, it's the moment I'm thinking about love and talking about love that I begin to think about him. Somehow, the four letters of love cannot exist without the four letters of his name, and I'm suddenly realizing the glaringly obvious emotions that have been sitting right under my nose demanding my attention.

I'm in love with him.

It hits me like a stack of bricks, forcing me out of my reverie, my fantasy land where we can stare at each other like two longing lovers in a Renaissance painting. I'm in love with Alex. and maybe I never stopped being in love with him, maybe it's always been in the back of my mind, lurking under resentment and anger and masquerading as hate. Maybe I've loved him for so long it's part of my soul, a splinter I can never dig out.

I'm in love with Alex Hernandez.

And that is not part of the plan.

I try not to let the dawning realization throw me off. I need to make it through the rest of this speech and make a *graceful* exit, not one that sends me tumbling down the stairs like a crazy person. I glance away from him, looking at a nice column to focus on as I get through the last few words.

Where was I? Oh, right. Love. "I'm so grateful that I've never felt like I had to choose, because I have loved and been loved both widely and deeply. I am so blessed to say that all the people I love, and who love me, have shaped me into who I am today and made this dream possible. So for all the ladies out there who feel like your dreams are far away, keep reaching. This is the moment before you become a supernova, and the galaxy is yours. Dream big."

When I reach the end of my speech, there's more applause. It's hard not to let my imposter syndrome take the wheel and question what I did to deserve this high praise I'm being given, but I manage to cast it aside. Like I said in my speech, this isn't about me. This is about a village of people who made it all possible.

I head back to my seat afterwards, and as I try my best to listen to the rest of the presentations, the other speakers at the ceremony, my head fills with white noise. I'm acutely aware of Alex murmuring to me, but whatever he's saying is drowned out by the rest of the room erupting with applause, engrossed in whatever's happening ahead of us.

I'm in love with him, and there's nothing I can do about it.

20

Alex

Olivia Sterling is a tough read.

I know she's excited about her win tonight. I know she's overwhelmed and grateful, and that she doesn't know how to navigate the spotlight but she does her best to be gracious and personable regardless, and no one is disappointed after speaking to her. As we navigate the rest of the ceremony, shaking hands and networking, I notice that she dodges my attempts to take her hand, to hold her arm. Even though we're introducing ourselves as friends, her body language is distant and cold.

She won't look at me.

I'm trying not to make this moment about me. Maybe I've made her nervous, maybe she doesn't want to get too caught up in me and neglect the company of other people. I don't want to spend too much time thinking about it and assuming her feelings, because Maya says assuming a woman's feelings is asking to get kicked in the nuts. I've never tested it, and frankly, I like my junk the way it is.

I am so proud of her that I don't know what to do with myself. I know how hard she's worked, how many nights she's stayed up studying, how much anxiety she's worked through, how many assholes she's told off. All of it has culminated in this achievement, and I know it's only the first of many awards she's going to receive over the course of her career.

She does a few short interviews, mostly giving quotes and comments and not dwelling too long on any single person. She floats around the room giving her undivided attention with so much sincerity, and as I watch her, I realize she's the most beautiful woman here, inside and out.

"Alex!"

When I turn around to see Ashley, one of my girlfriends from my early career (girlfriend being a very *loose* term. We were only together for a couple of weeks), I'm so startled I lose track of Olivia in the sea of people. She mentioned something about grabbing a drink, so I figure it's best to stay planted in case she needs to find me.

Ashley Chen is a fellow Berkeley alumn and a decorated journalist. I'm surprised she's here tonight, but I guess she must've relocated or decided to chase the story. I awkwardly return her hug, thrown off by the whole thing.

"Uh, hey!" I say. "How are you?"

"Pretty good," she replies. "I saw you're with Olivia Sterling, the Woman of the Year herself. Think you can talk her into giving me something for the SD Tribune?"

I chuckle. "Sure. I'll have to find her, but she's not being too cagey. I'm sure she'd be happy to talk."

"She's beautiful, you know," Ashley says. "You two make a beautiful couple."

"Oh, we're not..." I trail off, not sure how to play this off without sounding like an idiot. "We work together. I'm on the Board of Investors for Sterling Innovations and she's a family friend."

"The board?" Ashley echoes. She whistles low. "So I guess you've been taking off, then. I saw a profile about you in *The Wall Street Journal*. Impressive stuff."

I forgot about the WSJ interview. Hell, I don't remember half the appearances I've made. Usually, I'm riding the coattails of a friend or I happen to date someone famous enough to grace a tabloid. Livvy has star power. Me? Not so much. I consider myself to be pretty boring.

Boring, but a gifted businessman. That's how I do what I do.

"Thanks," I reply.

"Well, tell me about what you've been up to. I'd love to write profiles about some of the guests this evening, and the two of you are a power couple! What's on the horizon for you, Alex? Any speaking engagements?"

"I'm giving the commencement address at Harvard's business school next spring," I answer. "I'm also doing an interview with *Time* magazine about my Latino-American identity and how it's given me unique skills in a predominantly white world of business."

I also have a deal with HarperCollins to write a memoir in the works, but until the deal is formally announced and the proposal is finished, I've been keeping it hush-hush. I want to give enough details about me to satisfy Ashley, but I don't want to get carried away and steal the spotlight or detract from the guests of honor tonight.

"Anything else?" Ashley prods.

I think for a moment, and when I find a good way to bring things back to Sterling, I continue. "I'm going to be organizing a charitable effort to visit Haiti next year to build and open a medical clinic in an underprivileged area with the medical technology and research being presently conducted at Sterling Innovations, where I've recently joined the Board of Investors. But as much as I'd love to shine a light on my philanthropic interests, this isn't about me. This is about all of the amazing ladies here and the work they're doing."

Admittedly, I didn't read up on the other nominees for the 30-under-30 as much as I would've liked. It's been a busy month. From what I've gathered, and from what Livvy privately told me during the drive, they're all doing amazing things that deserve to be headlined too, and I don't want to undermine that. I mean, what good would that do?

Ashley smiles. "Well, if I can't catch up to her, I figure I need a failsafe. I'd love to hear about what drew you to Sterling. Anything in particular? What do you think is next for Olivia after this victory?"

The answer comes easily. "I think this is just the start of what is going to be an amazing career full of philanthropy and advancement in the medical technology field. I think she and Dominic are full of promise, and that potential for more success after all they've already accomplished at a young age speaks for itself."

"You sound like you really admire them."

"I do. I always have."

Finally, the crowd parts and Olivia comes into view. Our eyes meet, and hers shift towards the door. I catch the hint, politely squeezing Ashley's shoulder and dismissing myself from the conversation before she asks me anything else. Sure, she's nice, but reporters make me nervous.

Olivia and I meet outside of the convention center, met with the cool night air and the ocean just a few feet away. I can hear the waves, feel the wind and salt in the air. It reminds me a lot of home, even though we're miles away from the Bay. Californians generally fall into two categories: NorCal and SoCal devotees. I'm sure anyone can guess where us Balboa Boys fall.

"I got offered a job," she says with a laugh. "I don't know if it was serious, but... Wow. This isn't real. This whole thing."

Her cheeks are flushed, and she's rocking a bit on her feet. When we used to sneak booze in high school, Livvy would sing the greatest hits of the Beatles when intoxicated, and I find myself wondering how many drinks it takes to get her to that point as an adult.

"Did you have a couple drinks?" I ask, fighting a smile.

She counts on her fingers, shaking her head. "Mmm more than a couple shots. Starting to feel them now." And just like that, the opening notes of "Hey Jude" are being hummed under her breath as she kicks off her flats and attempts to steady herself.

"Oh good," I say sarcastically. "We better get you some Advil and water."

She shakes her head. "I want to enjoy the night for a bit. Out here, I mean. All of those people keep asking me questions and asking where I got my dress and I feel like any minute someone is going to take my trophy and tell me it was an elaborate prank."

"It would be a fucked up prank," I remark.

"Right?" She pushes a hand through her hair, shaking it loose from some of its pins. "God, I can't wait to put something comfortable on and watch TV. Do you think the hotel room has cable?"

The more the alcohol seems to be kicking in, the more bubbly she gets. She's talking faster than a sitcom character, and keeping up with her wild train of thought is almost an adventure in itself. I wasn't aware hotel cable could be so important to someone who's been drinking, but she proves me wrong.

"Probably," I say. They put us into a really nice hotel, so I'd assume the flatscreen is programmed with more options than a standard Holiday Inn. I don't use hotel TVs enough to care, but I'm aiming to be supportive. I take her trophy out of her hands, allowing her more range of motion to hold her arms out and take in the night breeze.

Her hair blows loose, and the sweat on her face dries. Her flush disappears, but two spots of red remain on her cheeks, and it's so adorable on her that I want to kiss her until she's blushing again.

It's an impulse I have to strike down. The more time I spend with her, the more they arise.

"It better be good cable," she says. "Most hotel cable is shitty."

"I... never really noticed."

She sighs. "That's how you boys always are. Never notice anything. Never, never."

I'm no genius, but that definitely felt a bit pointed, like she was trying to say something to me without outright saying it. I know I should take it with a grain of salt, but my curiosity gets the better of me.

"What?" I ask, confused. "Liv, what are you talking about?"

She waves her hand at me. "I shouldn't have said that. I'm a little drunk." She holds up her fingers, making a pinching gesture with them, leaving only the smallest space between her index finger and thumb. "Little, little bit."

If she's a only little drunk, then I'm next in line for the British throne.

"Uh-huh," I reply. "And does drunk Livvy want to tell me why you ditched me in there and have been acting weird since you got your award?" Maybe it's wrong of me to ask when she's like this, all unfiltered and ready to give me the truth. I can't help myself. It rolls out of my mouth before I can stop myself.

"Because I made a mistake!" she informs me. When intoxicated, she almost sounds like she's explaining quantum physics to a kindergartner. That's the best way to describe her voice at this moment, as she rattles off whatever uncensored feelings live inside her beautiful head. "I never should've come here with you, getting all confused with my feelings and making myself confused and upside-down and turned around."

Okay, she's more than a little drunk. She's very, very inebriated, and spinning around with her arms out like she's trying to fly. The gestures, the way she's acting it all out, feels a bit theatrical. I know she's a bit of a lightweight, especially with the way her body processes sugar and calories. I don't want to take whatever she's babbling about too seriously, but hope surges through me before I can think better of it.

Dammit. She always knows how to knock down my walls.

She stumbles a bit, reminding me not to get too lost inside of my own head.

"Hey, what's your sugar at?" I ask her. *Change the subject. Smooth, Alex.*

"Why do you care?" she fires back accusingly.

"Because you're rocking around and I'm trying to figure out if it's because your sugar is low or because you're drunk."

She reaches for her phone, squinting at the screen as she pulls up the app. "Both."

"Okay, let's get you something to eat."

She shakes her head. "I'm enjoying the air."

Alright. I'm glad she's having fun as the alcohol sits in her system and turns her brain to mush, but I'm starting to get a bad feeling about all of it, and it's probably good that we leave before drunk Livvy starts answering questions from the press. The moment people notice we're out here, they'll start trying to talk to her again. Maybe it's just me, but drunk interviews don't sound like a great idea.

I sigh. "You're going to faint and crack your head open and Dom will kill me. Please let me take you to get something to eat. It'll sober you up and fix your sugar. And save me from your brother."

She pokes my chest with her finger. "He'll already want to kill you for sticking your thing in me. It's okay, though. I liked it."

Wow. Okay. Not what I was expecting. "My... what?"

"Your thing," she says again, like avoiding the word "penis" is somehow better than saying it. "If he finds out, he'll be mad. But it was nice."

"Uh-huh, I know."

I think the sex review is nice, but it's definitely not something I want to be hearing right now, in public. I try to get her attention, but she starts humming "Hard Day's Night" and wiggling around in a pseudo-dance, oblivious to me and anything else.

She turns away from me, and finally, because I'm not sure what else to do, I scoop her off the ground, into my arms, and start to carry her to the car while she delivers off-key renditions of classic hits.

"Why are you Princess-carrying me?" she demands. Incidentally, she doesn't fight me. If anything, she seems to be enjoying it. I suppose that's why the question is less accusatory and more curious than anything else.

"Because you need to eat and you're drunk enough to twist your ankle again," I say. I do my best to ignore the smell of her perfume, the way she leans into my neck and sighs contentedly.

"You're a good man, Alejandro Hernandez," she whispers. "You know that?"

I don't know what to say to her, so I decide it's probably better to say nothing at all.

I hit the first drive through I can find, which happens to be In-N-Out: a California staple and one of her favorite places to eat. Drunk Livvy also makes a spectacular mess when she eats, but it's adorable, and I figure I can clean the spills later. She doesn't protest when I pay for the meal, which I'm relieved about. Instead, she just happily munches on her food and dips her fries in her strawberry milkshake.

"Everything is so messy now," she says to me, turning down the radio.

"What do you mean?" I pass her a napkin, assuming she means the insane amount of sauce and grilled onions smeared on her fingers. There's no graceful way to eat a double cheeseburger and a messy order of fries, and it's cute seeing her so unbothered about it.

"I mean with you and me. It's messy now," she says, repeating the word like it'll mean something different or more specific if she says it again. "I thought we could just be friends and then I thought we could handle sex and now... Now, I don't know."

She shoves a massive bite of her hamburger into her mouth, chewing and avoiding my eyes. I figure it's probably best to drop it while she's drunk, but there's so much unsaid, so much hanging in the air. *Sex? Friends?*

I don't want to get my hopes up. I know better than to do that. I know I don't deserve any more chances with her anyway, not after the history we have, and all the things I've done and the distance between us that's become insurmountable with age.

But, fuck, do I hope. Hope is a pesky little thing.

"Let's get you to bed," I finally say. I turn the engine over and start heading back towards our hotel, pretending the pit in my stomach is because I gorged myself on fast food and not because emotionally, I'm an ocean away from the woman I've loved since I was a kid, and yet, she feels closer than ever.

When Liv and I get back up to our room, she locks the door behind us and faces it, pulling the waves of her caramel hair over her shoulder to reveal the back of her champagne-colored gown. "Can you unzip me?"

Fucking hell. It's like the universe is playing games with me, taunting me with the forbidden fruit. I used to sit bored in church on Easter listening to the stories about Adam & Eve and the first sin, and now I'm starting to get why he bit the damn apple. I used to think he was an idiot, but Livvy makes me reevaluate it all. If it were her asking me, I'd give up paradise.

Maya says men are idiots. I'm definitely starting to see why she thinks so.

I pull her zipper down gently, trying to ignore the elegant dip of her back and the dimples at the base of her spine, which I got very acquainted with just last weekend as I bent her over the bed and fucked her senseless. *Jesus, Alex, get it together.*

"You're awfully think-y," she says, poking my bicep. "What's on your mind?"

"Liv, you're drunk, and I think you just need to get some rest. This can wait—"

"Alex," she pleads. "Just tell me. We're gonna be sharing a bed. Let's not make it awkward."

The confession slips out before I can stop it, before I can take it back. And maybe I should think better of it. Maybe I should stop myself. But the emotions I've been holding in are flooding out now, and it's late and I'm tired and I'm not drunk, but I've been drinking. Out it pours.

Nothing good happens after midnight. Or is it 2am? Whatever the saying, all I know is it's late, and I'm done hiding anything from her.

"I wish it had been you," I whisper. "My person. My wife. My one and only. I wish I could take it all back. I should've apologized before you went to Yale, tried long distance. I should've done…" *Everything, Liv. I should've done everything differently, and I didn't. And now I'm a man with regrets and so much love with nowhere to go.*

Livvy. My mind drowns in her name. *Livvy, Livvy, Livvy, why did I ever let you go?*

She turns, frowning at me. Her green eyes turn quizzical. "You think we would've worked out? Alex, you took my virginity and dumped me. Do you know what my friends said? They said you were just waiting for me to put out so you could end it. It wouldn't have mattered what you said or did. I would've hated you." She clutches the material of her dress tight to her chest. "I don't even… I don't know why we're talking about this."

She disappears into the bathroom. Thankfully, she doesn't slam the door, but it clicks into place firmly, assertively enough to send a message. I undo the knot in my tie, hoping the pressure will somehow let up from my chest, but it doesn't do a damn thing for me.

I may have just made everything worse. I probably did.

I know I've been drinking too. Definitely not as much as her, and after eating I doubt any of it is still in my system. So what's my excuse?

That you're a fool in love, Ben would say. He was always the most theatrical out of all of us, and after a stint in college theater and dabbling in Shakespeare, he's always full of vaguely poetic statements when it comes time for advice.

I change into my pajamas and take the furthest edge of the bed. As I wait for Liv, holding my breath, I debate throwing a pillow between us on the mattress, but I'm not sure she would think it was funny or charming. I'd rather not test the waters, not anymore than I already have tonight.

Finally, she stumbles into bed, collapsing under the mound of blankets with a long, heavy sigh.

"Goodnight," she mumbles, half-asleep, "Love you."

And then she's snoring before I can process what she's just told me. No matter how many times I turn it over in my mind, I realize I heard her exactly right the first time. She's drunk, and drunk people don't always mean the things they say, right? Or maybe they do, and I've got it all turned around in my head.

I fall asleep playing her sleepy confession over in my mind.

Love you. Love you. Love you.

What I never see coming is her absence. When I wake up in the morning, she's nowhere to be found. Her bags are gone, and all that's left is a note on the back of her business card saying *Flew home. Feeling sick. - Olivia*

And just like that, I realize this is how it feels to lose her all over again, and there's nothing I can do about it.

21

Olivia

I woke up when the alcohol wore off just after four in the morning, and when the memories of what I said to Alex hit me like a truck, including that treacherous, sneaky *I love you*, I did what I considered to be the only sensible thing in the world…

I booked an early flight with Dom's preferred private airline and was out of San Diego before sunrise. That's how bad this panic of mine was: I got over my fear of flying. Nothing mattered more than getting the fuck out of the same postal code.

I told Alex I was sick. By told him, I mean I wrote a note on one of my business cards and snuck out of the room because I was too ashamed of myself to face him. How could I look at the man I love and push him away? I know myself, and I know what I can and can't do. That firmly lies under the "can't" folder in my mind. Absolutely fucking not.

The weird thing is, I don't head back to my apartment, where Benedict Bridgerton awaits me. I'm faced with this horrible, spiraling moment of panic, and all I can think is: I need my brother. I don't have *I need my brother* moments often, but I find that when everything feels like it's going to shit, I know Dom usually has a solution.

So I turn up at his door. I've got bags wheeled behind me, and one of my shoes is only half on after the hasty escape I made from the hotel room, and I'm pretty sure I look nothing like my usual self, but I don't care.

When Dom answers, clearly shocked that I'm back on Sunday morning, unshowered, makeup smeared, and hungover, all he does is look me over. "Are you okay? Alex called. Said you were sick—"

Alex. Hearing his name sends a crack down the center of my heart, splitting me open down the middle, tearing me apart from the inside out.

I throw my arms around him, and I start to cry.

"Woah, okay." Dom might look like an intimidating member of the mafia, but he's always been soft for his family. He doesn't hesitate to hug me back, but he's definitely panicking at my sudden outburst of emotions, and when he asks me why I'm crying, I can't tell him, because I'm not even sure what I'm upset about.

Am I upset with Alex? Am I upset with myself for what I feel about him? Am I frustrated because I don't know? Am I PMSing?

Dom leads me into the apartment and guides me to the couch. The mini fridge in his living room is stocked with drinks for everyone who comes over, from Miles's favorite beer to my favorite LaCroix flavors. He passes me a drink, and he waits for me to gather myself.

"Where's Maya?" I ask.

"She went shopping. I told her I was going to have groceries delivered, but she insisted on going to Whole Foods herself and picking her own avocados," he answers. "The housekeeper's here though. Hey, Grace!"

"Hi!" Grace replies with a wave, disappearing into his office with the vacuum.

He doesn't have to ask me what's going on, or prompt me to get to the root of my feelings with precise questions. Dom and I have a brother-sister intuition that means words aren't necessary sometimes. He knows what I need, sometimes before I do.

"What happened?" he asks. "I swear to god, if Alex let something happen to you—"

"No," I say. "He didn't... Nothing *happened*. Well, not at the... It's complicated."

Dom's brows furrow. He gets to his feet, rubbing his temples. "Fucking hell. I know it was a date for charity, but don't tell me you two..."

"Not there. Not then." I bury my face in my hands. "Dom, I messed up."

My brother is the kind of guy who has a very short fuse when it comes to the people he loves. Even the implication of someone he cares about being hurt makes him murderous, and I know better than to assume there's any way to get this out without things getting explosive.

Dom chews his lip, his voice shaking with anger. When we were kids, he'd punch bullies on the playground for me, and even as grown-ups, that loyalty is fierce in him. His questions come so fast I can barely keep up. "What did he say to you? Did he touch you? I'll fire him and hire a guy to dump his corpse in the Bay and make it look like an accident—"

You know, Dom is a billionaire, and with the amount of money he has, I'm not sure his threats are entirely empty. He'd probably take someone out if he had to, and his bank account would barely change.

"Dominic! He's your best friend!" I interject.

"And you're my sister. I love the guy, but I'll fuck him up. Say the word."

"No," I say slowly. "Alex didn't do anything wrong. Are you going to be calm about this? Or do I need to go talk to someone else?"

"Talk to me," he replies. "I promise I'll try to keep an open mind."

I shoot him a look.

"I'll keep an open mind," he amends. "Better?"

"Much."

I trace a bead of condensation on the side of my can, trying to find the guts to spit the words out. I know it'll feel better once it's been said, but I don't know how to start. The hardest thing is always the beginning, the moment you start to climb.

"We slept together," I say finally. The whole sentence comes out in one word, one gasp like I'm trying to make a new sound entirely. "It wasn't supposed to be anything, but it opened up a lot of feelings for me. I got drunk last night, and I said some things, and I had to leave this morning because I fucked everything up."

Dom groans. After a moment he says, "Do you want me to talk to you like my business partner or my sister?"

"Um, both, I guess." After all, my personal life and professional life have decided to collide in a glorious mess of yarn, and I can't untangle it without help. Like it or not, this has become something both of us have to deal with.

Dom turns away from me, putting his face in his hands. After a breath, he scrubs one of them over his face, scratching absently at his jaw. "You understand how important Alex is to Sterling, right? I mean, he's half of the mind behind our budget proposal. The board now respects him more than anything, and we know the fuckers are loyal. We can't afford to lose anymore investors, and I thought you two could put aside all of your personal shit and just work together to benefit *both* of our businesses. I thought you were finally breaking ground. I didn't realize that meant fucking your coworker—"

"You're sleeping with Maya!" I exclaim.

"I shouldn't need to explain to you why that's a wildly different situation, because you know that yourself. We don't bring our relationship to work. I love you more than anything, but you two haven't done the best job of leaving behind the personal stuff. You're a smart woman, Liv, what were you *thinking*? You normally plan ahead a hell of a lot more than anyone, so why wouldn't you think this one through?"

"I don't know." Or maybe I do. Alex is my blind spot. He's the independent variable that throws me off my orbit like a fucking asteroid. He's a cosmic force. He's the one thing in my life I'd consider to be a wild card, and no matter what I do, it's always that way. It's an inescapable, relentless pattern. A bond that will never break. A cord that can't be cut.

"You need to figure out how to smooth this over," he says, "And I'm sure, assuming you didn't throw anything at him, whatever you said can be apologized for."

"I told him I love him."

Dom drops the glass of water in his hand. The glass shatters on the floor, and his housekeeper is there to clean it in a matter of moments. He thanks her profusely, trying to recover from his surprise.

"I thought you were going to tell me you said something mean to him or threatened to hit him with his own car," Dom says. "I didn't think… Fuck. *Do* you?"

"Do I…?"

"Love him?" he clarifies. "Are you in love with him?"

Logically, I know what the answer is. I know it the way

Bidding on Love

I know that 2+2 is 4 and Maya's favorite color is purple and my mom is fifty-nine this fall. I know I love Alex the way I know his eyes are brown, but painted with honey and whiskey. I know I love him the way I know his laugh, the new lines in his face, the tiny mole under his ear. I know I love him the way I know I breathe, and yet, when it comes time to turn my thoughts into words, I'd rather dissect my feelings than admit my own truth.

"It's not that simple," I say finally.

Dom sighs. When he's really frustrated, like he is right about now, he gets a line between his eyebrows that cuts his forehead deep, like his annoyance is a canyon. "Liv, this kind of thing is frighteningly simple. Love isn't something you can explain away or make excuses for or ignore. It just *is*. Like gravity or some shit. Some universal constant."

Like gravity or some shit. I hope he puts that in his vows. "Well, I do," I murmur. "But I can't. I can't love him. Even if he reciprocates my feelings—"

"He fucking better, if he put his cock in you."

"Jesus, Dom!" I choke on my own breath, reeling from what he just said. It's blunt and crass and honestly, kind of a gross image coming from a sibling. Normally, this kind of talk is a no-go, but it seems like all the usual rules are out the window.

I wait for him to chuckle, but he doesn't. Dom is way too serious sometimes. It's kind of unnerving. "I'm not kidding, Livvy. He better be willing to commit and treat you like a queen, or I'll castrate him."

I roll my eyes. "I think your girlfriend would probably be upset to hear you're threatening her brother's life."

"Or maybe she'd agree."

I doubt that one. I'm pretty sure Maya ships Alex and I, but I've never asked, and more importantly, have never wanted to. "I don't think so."

"Not the point!" Dom dismisses me with his hand, his voice raised in exasperation. "If you love him, then maybe that's not the worst thing in the world to confess. I mean, it always comes out, no matter how much you fight it. Love isn't a choice. Sometimes it's a thing that happens to you."

I've heard Dom say many times that the world would function so much better if he was in charge of it. Sometimes I wonder if that's true. Other times, I wonder if he'd just rather fix everybody's lives for efficiency's sake.

"I can't be with him," I say at last. "No matter what I want, or what I think I want. I can't."

"Why?" Dom demands.

"You don't remember?" I ask. I know it's been a while since we rehashed the story of our breakup and why everything is so strained, but surely Dom isn't that forgetful. I hate getting into it, but lately, it's a scab that keeps getting picked open.

I catch my breath, trying to keep myself from crying. I always cry when I'm frustrated, and it's annoying as hell. "God, he tore me apart. He took my virginity and then broke up with me right before the prom not even a day later. He broke my heart. He shattered it, actually. I haven't been able to give myself to anyone because I'm terrified of being hurt by someone I care about again. Why would I open up and give him the power to destroy me again? What if this is just another moment where he decides he's outgrown me and breaks me into a million pieces?"

There it is. All the pain I've been carrying, all the insecurity and commitment issues and worries. All of it bubbles to the surface and pours out. I feel like a bottle of coke that's been shaken too hard, and now I'm just bleeding all of my feelings out with reckless abandonment.

"I didn't know all that, and I'm so sorry you had to

carry that alone. But he didn't outgrow you," Dom says quietly.

"Then why did he leave?" I demand. "For fun?"

I don't know what I thought the answer was going to be, but when the words leave Dom's mouth, I'm finally hit with the twist I never expected, the stone I left unturned.

"Because you were going to give up Yale!" he snaps.

"What?" I ask.

I can't imagine a version of my life where I didn't go to Yale. I applied to other colleges because the counselors told me too, but I never planned on attending anywhere but Yale. It wasn't my top choice, it was the *only* choice.

But I guess, now that I remember it, I did get into Berkeley. And UCLA. And a few other places.

Did I ever really consider them? I mean, it's been well over a decade. I can't remember.

Dom sighs, and explains, "You got accepted into Yale and Berkeley, remember? Yale was your dream, and forever, you'd been so set on going. Except when the letters came in, you told him, told *us*, that you were going to think about it. You wanted to 'think' about your *dream school* and Alex knew it was because of him."

It comes back to me now in a clear picture. I did think about it. I was so young and so in love that for a moment, I thought about saying I got *rejected* from Yale to have my choice made for me, but Dom got the mail first.

He continues, "He knew you could do alright at Berkeley, but you belonged at Yale, and that it would open every door you needed. The connections you'd make. You had a full-ride. So, because he wanted you to have a real choice, because he wanted you to be a fucking Woman of the Year, he broke up with you, and he cried on the couch in Miles's basement all night."

The thought of Alex crying, being in pain the way I

was, sends a pang through my chest. Because he did the breaking up part, I assumed he'd moved on, that he wasn't hurt by the split. But now, I'm starting to see that I don't know a damn thing about his side of the story, and I feel like the biggest asshole on the planet.

"I didn't know that," I whisper. "How come you never... How come he didn't..."

"I couldn't tell you." Dom sighed. "The night it happened you came into my room and asked me what I knew. I told you I didn't know anything because he swore me to silence until you went off to school. He knew it would be easier for you to leave if you hated him, and after your first semester, you never asked me again. You were doing so well, and so Alex and I agreed to keep it between us guys."

When Alex called it off, I accepted Yale's offer and I never spoke to him again. After the breakup, I gave him the cold shoulder. I'd never asked my questions, and for the last several years, I'd forgotten them. I'd forgotten most of everything after, but not how it felt.

"So what do I do?" I ask finally.

"Fix this. Talk to him. Because it's about damn time."

22

Alex

I get back from San Diego late Sunday night. By the time I'm dragging myself up the stairs, I'm cursing every traffic god for making the trip more miserable than it had to be, and I'm pissed at Livvy for making me drive down there in the first place only to take a damn flight back.

Ten hours, twelve hours, however long my purgatory behind the wheel was—It gave me plenty of time to think about everything. By the time I'm carrying my bags up to my apartment, ready to relieve the dog sitter, I have a clear head.

Here's what I know, I tell myself. *I'm in love with Olivia. Olivia might be in love with me. I don't know how we're going to keep working together, and I don't know how either of us can have space without sabotaging the company.*

When I open my front door, the last thing I'm expecting is for Olivia to be sitting on the couch with the dogs laying beside her. Immediately, they rush to the door to greet me, and she stands, hesitant.

"I can explain," she says.

"Please do. Because otherwise, I'm going to assume you

broke into my apartment to… keep my dogs company?" I snort. Whenever I'm being ambushed by adorable rescues, it's hard to be aloof and standoffish. They have that effect on me.

"I was going to wait outside for you to get home," she explains, "But then the dog sitter saw me on the front door camera and assumed I was here to relieve her, so she let herself out and I couldn't just leave the dogs alone, they seemed so sad, so we've been watching *Buffy* reruns and snuggling."

It's cute when she talks fast like that. It's even cuter that she stayed with my dogs so they wouldn't be lonely, even for a couple of hours. It's such an Olivia thing to do that my heart aches with affection for her.

God, how could I be so stupid? How could I ever be in the orbit of Olivia Sterling and not be head over fucking heels for her?

"So why are you here?" I ask her. "I doubt the plan was to hang out with my dogs, so why are you really here?"

"We need to talk," she says.

"I agree." But no one wants to hear the words *we need to talk*. They're usually weighty and intense and mean something very unpleasant is waiting on the other side of them. I feel like I'm holding my breath, waiting for her to make or break the situation.

"I'm sorry," she begins, "I shouldn't have gotten as drunk as I did for a number of reasons, the least of which being the fact it was a professional event and beyond that, because I'm not your problem and you shouldn't have to babysit me."

So far, this isn't a world-ending conversation. I take it as a win, though my own anxiety has my heart beating in my ears. Her words are almost muffled because of it. I wasn't expecting an apology for drinking, and all things considered, it was a special occasion, a celebration. She deserved to have fun, and I'd happily babysit her anytime.

Still, it seems like she needs to say it, so I let her. It seems like she has plenty she needs to say, and while I'm not sure I want to hear it, I'm certain I don't have another choice. I love her too much to silence her, and I want to know too much not to hear her out.

She looks as exhausted and miserable as I feel. I don't know what that makes me feel. A million instincts rush through my mind, and none of them stick.

"And I'm sorry for the stuff I said. I unloaded a lot of incoherent bullshit on you and I wouldn't have if I'd been less drunk and holding on to my self-control," she continues. "Look, I don't want this to affect our working relationship. I know my *issues* are mine, and we don't need to doom Sterling with our teen angst bullshit, so—"

"So that's what this is about? Work?" I demand.

It's a blow. It reminds me of the first time I got into a fight in middle school, how it felt to take a right hook to the jaw. It hits that hard, and it takes my breath right out of my chest. My stomach sinks low. I thought I'd spent a car ride mourning, but this is a new low.

Part of the reason I've avoided dating is because I never wanted to be the kind of man who's pursued exclusively for my wallet. It's become an issue too many times. I just never thought that Olivia would ever care more about my money than me. Never her. Others maybe, but never her.

"What else would it be about, Alex?" she whispers, at a loss. Maybe she doesn't read my hurt. Maybe she's too consumed by the script she's undoubtedly come up with before coming here.

I feel like I've blown up the walls I built around my

feelings, and all of them are rushing out of me like a sea of violent water.

"Us?" I start. With each breath, each word, I lose more of my control. It rushes out of me, raw and honest. "What you said about your feelings for me?"

At this point, I don't care about tiptoeing. I don't care about dancing around her feelings and trying to be delicate because she's shown me that delicate doesn't do shit. Being Mr. Nice Guy doesn't help me either. At the end of the day, I'm the chump who loses the girl, and it seems like the girl is slipping through my fingers like sand no matter what I say, what I do.

I feel so helpless. Very rarely am I confronted with problems I can't solve, but here's one glaring in front of my face like breaking news.

Fuck it, I think to myself. "Maybe if you showed up here ready to admit you got too real and are now chickening out, this would be better. But instead, all you care about is the fucking company."

She doesn't deny it. That's the worst part. I spend a second waiting for her to tell me that's not the truth, to interrupt me before I spiral, but she doesn't. My hope swells and then crashes, and then evaporates in a single moment. Maybe I didn't think she'd say anything, but I wanted her to. I wanted so *badly* to be wrong.

"Really, Olivia?" I demand. "What about me? What do I get in return for putting up with the push and pull and the on and off. One minute, you like me and we're flirting and I even think we're getting somewhere, and the next, you're disappearing in the middle of the night! What am I supposed to do with that, Livvy? I have feelings too."

Livvy. Fuck, saying her name is like swallowing a handful of razor blades. The nickname is a habit I need to break, because it crushes me, renders me a pile of shards I'll only cut myself on.

"I never meant to hurt you, Alex," she whispers. Her face is so stricken with sorrow and grief that I almost believe her. I want to believe her.

But I don't.

I'm not a stupid kid with naive ideas about love anymore.

Besides, time and time again she's assumed the worst of me. I don't know how she turned me into a villain in her head after all this time, but at every chance I've tried to do the right thing, she's taken it as an attack, anticipating the worst outcome, assuming the worst intentions on my behalf.

"Well, you seem to think I mean to hurt you," I seethe. "You've let me know plenty of times what you think about me. Like somehow, my teenage mistakes are the only thing that defines me. I get it, I was shitty, but you're not perfect either, Olivia, and it doesn't matter how many times I've tried to make it up to you, you'd rather make me your bad guy!"

My voice cracks. I'm so humiliated I turn away from her.

The dogs whimper, confused why we're arguing, unsure of who to comfort. For a moment, I'm more upset at her for initiating this conversation in front of them than I am at her for having it at all.

"That's fair. You're right to be mad at me." She doesn't fight me. She doesn't argue. If anything, she seems completely defeated, resigned to my judgment.

"Yeah, I am," I retort. "Look, if you want me to resign, I will."

After the week I've had, after the *weeks* I've endured of roller coaster emotions trying to figure out what she wants from me, what she feels, I'm ready to give up. Whatever ends my misery. Whatever makes this a cleaner break instead of a series of jagged cuts that remind me of old wounds and old hurt.

She shakes her head. "No. You're too important to Sterling, and Dom needs you. If anyone should quit, it's me. I can take the job in San Diego and you can be the new CFO. The board likes you better anyway."

"You're not quitting." I scoff. She's being ridiculous. I don't know what world she thinks Sterling functions without her in, but I know it doesn't exist, and anyone with half a brain would feel the same way.

"And neither are you!" she exclaims. "God, Alex, why is your instinct to run away from everything?"

Because sometimes, it's the only way to lessen the pain for everyone involved. Or even because it's the only thing I know how to do half the time.

"I don't see how we have another choice," I reason. I mean, isn't it obvious? This isn't working, and when something isn't working, it's insane behavior to keep pushing, trying to make something out of nothing, to spin gold where there's nothing but twine. I'm not a masochist, and there's no world in which this works out keeping the status quo.

Doesn't she get that? Do I really have to tell her why?

"Why not?" she demands.

Fucking hell. She's gonna make me say it. The challenge is in her eyes, lightning cracks across the green of her irises, and I know she's pushing me intentionally. Maybe I deserve it, but it drives me insane.

And it makes me want to kiss the hell out of her, which is absolutely not the right move in this situation. Thank god I'm not thinking with the downstairs head, because otherwise I'd be diving headfirst into a number of piss-poor decisions.

And so I say the words. I say them because this is my Hail Mary, because I can't keep it in anymore. I say the words because I've got nothing else in me, and she's pushed the last button.

"Because I'm in love with you, Olivia!" I explode. "Because every time you're around me, I forget how to think clearly. Because every moment that I am apart from you, I feel like I'm being ripped apart, like someone has amputated one of my limbs. It tears me up to be away from you. It's even harder to be around you and know that I can't touch you, talk to you, tell you precisely what you mean to me. So no, I *can't* work with you. I can find a way to work remotely, the way the other investors do. But I can't breathe your air and pretend it isn't killing me!"

I know I'm on the verge of tears. I don't make a habit of crying in front of women. It's not a toxic masculinity thing so much as a habit, a universal strategy for keeping my guard up. I look away from her to breathe a little easier, to grasp at any semblance of control, as if I can stop myself from falling apart.

She's quieter now as she speaks. I try not to imagine what her face looks like, but I know her expressions well. Too well. "But what about—"

I can't listen to her anymore. The sound of her is like nails in my coffin. "Dom has run his own business for a long time. My ideas aren't going to make or break it."

I need her to leave. I can't keep running in circles trying to do something different when I know the end result. I know what's going to happen if I keep fighting her, and it's too late to undo all the damage she's done, or the damage I've done.

She wants her fucking company. All that matters is her

job, and she's told me that time and time again. I've just been a shitty listener.

"It's all about my money apparently," I say. I laugh, but there's no humor in the sound. Just an empty, hollow noise. "Don't worry, you have it. That's what you wanted, right? To keep your damn job? To keep the company afloat? I never thought you would be capable of being such a cold, heartless shell, but apparently, we don't know each other at all anymore."

"Alex—" she pleads. Her voice breaks, and it hits me hard, but I'm drowning and I need to come up for air.

"Don't fucking worry, Olivia, I'll write you a check for whatever fucking dollar amount you want if it means I never have to see you again."

I leave her alone in the living room, sitting in my bathroom with my hands braced against the counter as silent, shuddering sobs wrack my body. I hate crying, but this is one situation where it rushes out of me before I can fight against it or even process what's happening.

When the front door slams shut, announcing her departure, I finally let myself fall apart for the second time in my life at the hands of Olivia Sterling.

My apartment feels more like a haunted house now that she's left.

The smell of her perfume is on the sofa. The dogs whimper and glance around, wondering why she left so abruptly without saying goodbye. I'm almost angry at her for bonding with them because it's made me love her more, and then I'm angry because there's no way to explain to a dog what it means to break up with someone.

If we can even call this a breakup.

This sure as shit isn't conducive for clearing my head or finding any semblance of emotional space, so I harness Tuck and Lily and head out to my SUV to take them down to the pier.

My yacht, *Sirius,* named after the dog star and immortalizing my love of canine companions, is docked at the marina with a few other privately owned boats. I keep it stocked with fine whiskey and a wine cellar with aging bottles of merlot, which is more for my mom than it is for me. Whenever life feels like it's a little too much, I take to the sea. The smell of salt and the lashing waves knocking against the side of the hull comfort me for reasons I don't entirely have words for. Something about being on the open water, surrounded by nothing but open space—possibility, one might even say—makes me feel a little more balanced in the grand scheme of things.

I'm about to take off when I hear Dom's voice calling from the dock. "Hey, Hernandez!"

Of course, Tuck barks excitedly from his perch on the front of the boat, his tail wagging when he recognizes Dom. Of all of my friends, Dom has always been his favorite. Maybe it's the fact he's around the most often, or maybe it's just that Dom shares his food more than anybody. Either way, he's always overjoyed to see him around.

I step out of the captain's quarters and sure enough, Dom is standing on the pier in blue jeans and a white button-down, looking more casual than I've seen him in a long time. He lifts his hand to wave, rocking forward on his loafers.

"I come in peace," he says. "Just want to talk."

"And why should I let you aboard?" I ask.

"Because you have my word that I won't punch you for sleeping with my sister," he offers. "Besides, I'm your best friend. Aren't I supposed to be here for your girl trouble?"

"Girl trouble?" I retort. "Is that what we're calling it now?"

Even still, I let him aboard.

It was Dom who taught me how to sail, actually. When Miles bought his first boat and nearly capsized us, Dom decided to teach us all how to navigate the waters without getting anyone killed. He was the first of us to be making billions, but even when his salary started with *m* he was hellbent on being generous with his time and resources. Now, three out of four of us Balboa Boys have boats; Ben gets motion sick and prefers to stay on land.

"So you talked to Liv?"

"And then she talked to you," he confirms. "And from what I hear, it didn't go very well."

"Well, she wants to make sure things are copasetic for the sake of the company, and I'd rather be with the woman I love, but apparently my money is more important than my feelings on the matter." I wince. "I know she's your sister. I don't want to make it sound like I'm calling her a gold digger or something."

"It's my fault," he says.

I pause. "What?"

"It's my fault she was so concerned with the company, the job, all of that," he clarifies. "I made sure she knew the impact it would have if the personal aspects of your relationship started to interfere with work. You know why I asked you to join Sterling, and yeah, maybe it's a little humiliating that I have to ask my best friend to clean up my mess, but you're an asset to the team, and having you around has made both Maya and I happier than I can find the words for."

I think back to the conversation Liv and I had, how

things played out. Maybe it did sound a little like Dom's words being parroted through her mouth. Admittedly, I hadn't considered that, but maybe I should've. Dom and Liv are closer than Maya and I, which says a lot. The two of them have always had their own sort of language, a bond I can't explain. He's her older brother, and what he thinks is so important to her.

Maybe that's why she led with the stuff about work. It wouldn't shock me if Dom was a part of the equation.

"Aren't you supposed to punch me or something? For getting with your sister?"

"My *adult* sister is more than capable of making her own choices," Dom replies. "And honestly, I did want to fuck you up a little, but I realize how hypocritical that would be. I mean, hell, I want to marry your sister—"

"Marry?" I cut him off. "Really?"

He nods sheepishly. "I was actually going to ask your blessing to propose after we talked about you and Liv."

"You have it," I say.

"And you have mine," he says back. "Look, I know you and Liv have a complicated history. I was angry at you for getting involved with her again because I was scared you'd break her heart, and honestly, anyone hurting Liv terrifies me. But the more I thought about it, the more I realized you two brought out the best in each other, and you made her happier than I've ever seen her. Even now, when she's pissed at you, there's a light in her eyes again that I haven't seen in forever. What kind of brother would I be if I didn't encourage the two of you to chase that happiness?"

Miles has always been evasive with his feelings, and getting him to admit anything close to emotionally vulnerable is impossible. Ben grew up in a "boys don't cry" household and has been unpacking the repercussions of that in therapy for a few years. But Dom was never that way, and neither am I. We've always been able to talk about everything, and even now, when I feel like a scab picked open, I don't feel like I have to hide anything.

"Well, I think you have one thing wrong," I say at last.

"Which is?"

"Liv doesn't feel that way about me," I reply.

"She does, you fucking idiot," he says with a groan. "It's kind of obvious. I'm embarrassed I missed all the signs, to be frank with you."

I snort. "Look, dude, you don't have to—"

"I do," he cuts me off. "The two of you are so dense you're going to keep skating around your feelings when you could just be happy. Get your head out of your ass, okay? Because if you need to break my sister's heart again, it better be for a good reason instead of *she loves me, she loves me not* bullshit."

I snort. "You really have a way with words, D."

"I know," he replies, "I could be the fucking president. Now don't just stand there—let's crack open a new bottle of scotch and watch the football highlights."

There's still a lot that isn't accounted for. A lot to say, a lot to unpack, but this is a start. Honestly, knowing Dom isn't plotting my murder takes a weight off, and once I get through my initial hurt, I know I have to talk to Liv. Whatever happens, happens.

But right now, I'm going to drink a thousand dollar bottle of scotch with my best friend.

"I can make that happen."

23

Olivia

Christmas doesn't feel the same this year.

I want it to. I want to pretend everything is business as usual, but it's not. Thank god the year is coming to a close so soon, because I need a serious detox, maybe a juice cleanse for my skin and energy levels and a recommitment to running a 5k and ridding myself of all the boy drama. Whatever it takes to get through this and remember who I am, or who I was before I let myself completely derail.

My family likes to keep things small. While I have an army of cousins who I'm sure would love to ask Dom and I for money, it's nice to just keep the holiday between the four of us. Well… the four of us, and Maya's family.

Which unfortunately includes Alex.

Seeing him after our fight was horrible. The fact he won't look at me all through dinner and present exchanging is even worse. He stays on the opposite side of the room at every turn, and when I try to catch his eye, he evades it expertly.

I want to tell him he's got it all wrong. I want to tell

him that I wasn't trying to put Sterling before his feelings or mine. Hell, I was assuming my crush was unreciprocated, that I was the one letting lines blur. I didn't want to make him uncomfortable. I didn't want to make him feel like he was somehow responsible for my emotions.

But I made a terrible miscalculation, and in doing so, I made everything So. Much. Worse.

I think I'm doing a semi-okay job of pretending everything is fine. The bags under my eyes speak for themselves, and I have a stressful job, so no one ever questions me looking a little under rested. Unfortunately, things between Dom and I are tense, and things between Dom and Alex are tense, so everyone is on eggshells trying to figure out what happened and how to fix it before the three of us start World War Three.

It's only happened one other time in the history of our families. It was some kind of middle school debacle, and it ended with Alma spraying all of us with a hose in January until we apologized to each other.

Hopefully, we can avoid the hose spraying this time around. I'd like to think now that we're adults things can be a tad more civil, but I also don't think I should hold my breath on that one. Alma is a woman no one trifles with.

After the wrapping paper has sufficiently covered the carpet and enough spiked eggnog has been passed around, Dom clears his throat. "Alright, everyone. I remembered one more present I've been, well, waiting to give. As everyone, Maya included, knows, things at Sterling have been crazy this year, and honestly without her, I think I would've lost my mind. Liv's always been my support at work, but Maya's there for everything, every moment, and I'm forever grateful to her for keeping me steady when I don't know how."

Is he finally doing it? I know Dom has been carrying a

ring for Maya in his pocket for months, but the timing was never right, and he wanted to make sure it was perfect for her. I'm sure Alex has already given his blessing.

"Maya," Dom says softly, in that voice he uses only for her. "You are the love of my life. You challenge me, and you care for me in ways I don't deserve, but I will spend the rest of our lives being the man you need and more. I love you more than anything."

He drops down to one knee. My mom starts to cry. Alma cups her hands over her mouth. Even Alex and my dad are smiling.

And my eyes are full of happy tears because my brother is happier than I've ever seen him before. And more than anything, he deserves it.

"Will you marry me?" he asks.

"Yes!" Maya exclaims. "Yes, I'll marry you!"

As they kiss and embrace and everyone claps and takes photos, Alex's eyes meet mine between camera flashes.

And in them, I see nothing but hate.

"What the fuck was Maya talking about?" I mutter under my breath. Hours into the evening, after our parents have become wine drunk and the engagement has made it to Facebook official status, Maya tells me she needs me to grab something from her overnight bag, since she and Dom stayed over to make my mom breakfast this morning.

I'm not sure why she insisted on having *me* do it. But hey, since she's newly engaged, I assume that comes with some kind of special privileges I'm not really privy to yet. As I kneel in front of her duffle bag, I catch on to her scheme a minute too late.

Alex steps into the room, "Hey, D—"

Our eyes lock. The door slams shut and locks from the outside.

When Dom and I were babies, we used to make great escapes out of bed, and since my parents have a steep staircase that could send any toddler to an early grave, they installed a child lock on the top of the guest room door frames (formerly our bedrooms). Apparently, those locks are still in place.

Alex knocks on the door hard. "What the fuck?"

"We're not letting you out until you make up!" Maya says through the heavy door. "It's for your own good!"

"Does Dom know about this?"

"Yes," my brother calls out, "And if you damage my mother's door, I'll kill you."

"I can pay for it."

"You can't make her cry on Christmas!"

He's got a point, as much as I hate to admit it.

"I'm gonna kill them," he says, slumping onto the bed.

I'm still planted firmly on the carpet near the closet, my head on my knees. Great. This is absolutely what I needed. Really channels the spirit of Christmas. Nothing says "Happy Holidays" like being held hostage to spend mandatory time with someone who despises you.

"I'm sorry, I didn't know Maya was scheming."

"I assumed she'd give up on her Christmas pranks now that she's about to be a married woman." Alex scoffs, pinching the bridge of his nose. "Apparently, not. I underestimated her. I underestimated *both* of them."

"I thought you and Dom were mad at each other," I say.

"No, we figured out shit out a few days ago when he asked my blessing to marry my sister. Things have just been awkward because you and I haven't worked it out yet. I guess this is a hell of a way to force our hands."

"It's definitely *one way* of doing things."

We both laugh despite ourselves. And it feels good. It feels right, the way we can bounce off of each other and talk, even when we're at odds.

"Look, Alex, can we talk?"

He looks at me, but doesn't say anything and I take his silence as permission to continue.

"It was never about Sterling. I mean, it was, but only because Dom was pissed at me for all the risks to the company. All I could think about was you until he reminded me how selfish I was being for not considering—"

"I know," he says softly. "He told me everything. I mean, it doesn't mean I wasn't hurt, but I guess I understand now why you led with all the work stuff. I was a dick, and I assumed, and I jumped to conclusions too fast, and that wasn't fair of me. Honestly, I've been an ass, and I'm tired of it, and I'm so forever fucking sorry."

"He told me about why you broke up with me when we were kids. The real reason. How come you never told me it was about Yale?"

"Because it was easier for you to hate me than to hope you could ever… that we could ever…" He trails off. "Forget it."

"No," I whisper insistently. "I can't just forget it. I can't just erase you from my life and act like I'm not hopelessly, completely in love with you."

This is another one of those moments, I realize. One of those earth-shaking, life-changing moments where everything falls into place, where something important is going to happen, and I need to follow my gut, because it's too important not to.

"Just, don't break my heart again," I whisper, "Because I've been in love with you my whole life, and I don't know what I'm going to do if I have to lose you all over again. Alex, you said you wished it could've been me, but for me, it's always been you. There's never been anyone else, and I'm not sure there ever will be."

He sighs, pinching the bridge of his nose. His head shakes in disbelief. "You mean that?"

"Yes," I whisper. "*Yes.*"

I don't know how I move so fast, or how he does. We surge forward, and under the mistletoe Maya so obviously placed, I kiss him until the space between us dwindles from inches to centimeters to nothing. I kiss away every ounce of sadness, every moment of miscommunication, every terrible memory where we both drew blood. I know you can't use a kiss to heal someone, not entirely, but I start to believe it may just be possible when I'm kissing Alex Hernandez. This feels like a beginning.

He tastes like hope, spiced rum, and endless tomorrows.

When we finally break apart, staring at each other and searching the other's face as if memorizing it, it's obvious we can never go back. Not from this, not from the point of no return we've so obviously reached. Finally, we've wound up where we're meant to be. And I'll be damned if I miss it.

Reaching for me again, he runs his hand down my neck, up my arm and over my shoulder, then down my throat and across my collarbone, ultimately settling on my cheek and gripping my face with his his fingers. His hands are rough from his workouts but gentle on my skin, and there's nothing quite like the scratch of his stubble as he kisses me. He's just close enough to be warm and electric, like lava in my veins, and I can't even breathe, dizzy from his proximity, and it's the most exhilarating ache of desire I've ever had in my life.

I steady myself in his arms, resting my hands on his chest. My back meets the edge of the bed, my skirt pooling on the mattress, and he leans forward.

"I think we're at an impasse," he says.

"So we are," I say back.

We're so close that our noses brush when we speak, and we're sharing breath between kisses. It's not like we haven't kissed before, or even had sex, but this is different. This feels different, and neither of us can get enough of it.

"I want nothing more than to be inside of you right now," he murmurs. His voice is gruff and thick with desire. "But we have to be quick, and we have to be really quiet. I'll take my time with you when we get back to your place tonight, and I'll make love to you until neither of us can stay awake."

I groan as he kisses my throat, nibbling at the skin and tracing patterns with his tongue. His hand comes up to cover my mouth, silencing me. It's sexy, the thrill of being caught.

When his mouth curves around mine again, his lips soft and demanding at the same time, I kiss him back. I revel in the feeling of the hard muscles in his chest, wishing I had time to caress every ridge. His cock is bulging through the seam of his pants, and I grind myself against it, eager to feel him inside of me.

My nipples are hard peaks underneath my thin dress. I didn't feel like wearing a bra, and I barely noticed before now. His hand slips down from my face, and slowly, he takes my breast into his palm and begins to work my nipple through the fabric with his thumb in slow circles.

"How wet are you?" he rasps. "Do I need to taste you, or are you ready for my cock?"

"I'm ready," I whimper. "Please."

His mouth travels lower, sucking and nipping at my

neck after he leaves my lips. I gasp, threading my fingers through his hair, whispering his name. *I don't want to stop.* I've pulled his tie undone and loose around his neck in the time it's taken to undo his belt.

I yank the knot of his tie free, casting it aside somewhere in the room. I kick aside my panties, lifting my skirt to give him access, because I know we don't have a lot of time to do this, and I'm desperate to be close to him. I want to feel him now, and maybe it makes me greedy that I'm not willing to wait, but I don't care.

He reaches down, stroking my clit with his thumb. He rubs me in slow strokes, and my knees almost buckle. "My good girl," he says. "You feel so good, baby. I bet you'll feel even better when I'm fucking you."

I pull his belt through the loops of his slacks, then he lets me tug them down just enough to free his massive length. His cock, huge and veiny, is hard in his hand. He strokes himself, pre-cum weeping through the head of his dick. When my hand touches him, he shudders, moaning my name into my hair.

Finally, he sits down on the edge of the bed and pulls me over him so that I'm straddling him. He frees my tits from the top of my dress, letting the straps fall away so he can take one of my breasts in his mouth. As he sucks my nipples, my eyes roll back.

"Alex, please. Please fuck me."

"You don't have to beg, baby," he whispers, "My cock is yours."

He runs his fingers along my pussy, teasing me with the head of his cock inside of my slit. He's so big, and especially at this angle, I can feel his size, and my body is aching for him, as if we've missed the pleasure of fucking him over the last two weeks. God, do I want him.

He gets about an inch inside of me, and I gasp. He stops, grinning. "We have to be quiet, baby."

I nod, biting my lip to stifle my noises. My eyes close, and he kisses my throat as I sink down on top of him. I just want to know how much of him I can take in this position, feel him reach every inch of my pussy. I want to know my limit, take his cock so deep I can't walk tomorrow morning.

Impatiently, I slam my hips down and fill myself with him. He moans so loudly into my shoulder I laugh, but the sound dies quickly as he begins to push in and out of me, fucking me fast and hard.

"Is this okay?" he asks. "God, you feel amazing."

"It feels good," I say, assuring him with a touch of my hand to his chest. I bounce my hips to meet him, up and down, fast and hard. I can't get enough of him, and I like that he's being rough with me, taking no prisoners as he slams his cock inside of me.

"So good," I gasp. I feel like a porn star with the whining sounds I'm making. We're doing a good job of being quiet, I'd say, and it's sexy, the thrill of possibly getting caught, knowing at any time someone could overhear. I'm breathless, moaning in his ear, feeling his sounds against my skin as he fucks me.

"Mmm, I want to feel you more."

Before I can ask what he means, he flips us so that I'm on my back and he's over me, careful not to crush me under his weight.

He's so careful as he moves in and out of me at first, trying to figure out if the bed is going to creak from the motion. When it doesn't, he's happy to move at our previous pace, going harder and deeper with each stroke. Our hips are rolling together and the sound of naked skin against skin is all I can hear. He reaches out, holding my chin up so that I'm looking into his eyes as our bodies come together over and over again.

He reaches one set of fingers down so he can begin stroking my clit as he drives me deeper into the mattress. "There you go, baby. I want to make you come. I want you to milk my cum out of me. I want to feel your pussy get tighter. I want to make you feel good, baby. Fucking come for me."

I'm mewling, crying out and wrapping my legs around him tighter, my thighs clenching and the fabric of my dress falling around us. I want him to pound me deeper, to claim me in a way only he can. There's something beautiful about learning sex with someone, and I want to learn it with him. "I'm so close," I whisper. "God, I'm so close."

"Come for me, baby," he orders. "I love you, baby, come for me."

And I do.

I tip over the edge, trembling as he continues to slam in and out of my cunt until he spills his own release inside of me.

We lay there for a moment, in stunned silence, catching our breath. It'll be a little conspicuous if we're gone for too long, so I know there's no real time for cuddling and aftercare, but we take a few moments to hold hands and breathe the moment in. Then, we find pieces of each other's clothes and get dressed.

He kisses me slowly and deeply, fixing his own clothes. "How do I look?"

"Like you just railed the shit out of me," I reply.

He snorts. "We're pretty obvious, huh?"

"I'd say so."

"You know I love you, right?" he whispers.

"I love you, too."

As we get our bearings, I text Maya to let her know she can unlock the door. While we wait, he takes my hand, and everything in the world feels like it's falling into place.

"What happens now?" I ask.

"Let's start with making up for too much lost time," he says.

Epilogue

Alex

A few months later...

This party is a bearable one, I'd say. Considering parties are not my thing, it's a big compliment. So far, neither Olivia nor I are looking for a quick escape, and the gathering is so full of light and laughter that I almost wish the afternoon could last forever.

Ninety percent of the time I err on the side of caution when it comes to events my sister plans. She has a tendency to invite too many people or some other mistake that leads to some last minute rearranging. Usually it turns out okay, but there's a lot of stress in the moments leading up to the final moment of resolution. This time, Gia and Liv help, but she still gets to lead.

Livvy and I offered to plan and host their engagement

party, but Maya was insistent on deciding on everything and Dom figured it was best to let her go nuts and do all the planning. He's a wise man for knowing better than to argue with her. They reserved the roof of their luxury apartment building for the occasion, and everything fell into place from there.

I know Livvy didn't want Maya to plan her own engagement party unless she was absolutely certain that she wanted to. I think at the end of the day both of us were relieved, since neither of us particularly enjoys party planning (or parties in general for that matter).

Maya's beautiful ideas come to life here, especially with help from her girlfriends. Seeing as she always creates beautiful celebrations just by being there, I'm not surprised, but the rooftop is an oasis of beauty. She's got all kinds of plants and floral arrangements decorating every bare surface, an all you can eat buffet that is as diet inclusive as humanly possible, photos of them developed on film and pinned to a clothesline that overlaps with the outdoor string lights that turn on at dusk, and so much color. I know her Pinterest boards are thorough, and that vision has completely come to life here.

Maya is wearing a gorgeous white mini-dress to commemorate the occasion. Dom, surprisingly, has been talked into wearing a tropical inspired Hawaiian shirt, probably to keep with the beach theme of their wedding. I'm shocked my sister got him to wear anything other than a suit or a black shirt, but sure enough, he's decked out in color and sunglasses. All of us are sneaking looks of surprise I'm sure.

There's a genuine mix of close family and friends on the rooftop this afternoon. Now that springtime has added a few new blossoms to the dreary San Francisco Bay and granted us a few sunny days here and there, we're able to gather outside and celebrate their engagement. The wedding is in the Maldives in the summertime, and that guest list is even smaller than this one.

Still, it includes the usual suspects: our parents, the Balboa Boys, and Gia, who along with Maya and Livvy, has formed a dynamic trio that could either #GirlBoss its way towards world peace or take over the planet. I'd say it depends on the time of the month, but I'd prefer to be alive and I suspect that joke wouldn't land well.

"I never thought Dom would tie the knot," Livvy admits to me, as we stand near the edge of the roof, looking over at the city and the endless blue on the horizon. "Until he found Maya, it seemed impossible."

"My mother is just excited that they might give her a grandchild soon," I remark.

Liv snorts. "Does *Dom* know about that part? Because I'm pretty sure he wants nothing to do with fatherhood anytime soon. He barely knows how to do his own laundry."

"I don't think he knows," I say. "He gets it sent out. He says it's to save time, but I've never seen that man fold anything in his entire life."

"You're one to talk. Everything you fold has wrinkles." At my offended expression, she lets out a laugh, and then a snort. "I'm sorry, baby, but it's true. It's why I do the laundry."

Most of the time, we have a housekeeper and a maid come in to do chores, but for whatever reason, Livvy insists on doing her own laundry whenever she has the chance. It's the strangest thing, but my favorite thing about her is her independence. I wouldn't change it for the world.

I frown at her playfully. "Excuse me. I didn't realize you were so upset with my folding abilities."

"With all the love in my heart," she says, "You're almost as helpless as Dom is."

I try to think of a quick comeback, but nothing good comes to mind. I'm sure I'll give her an earful later, since we've always been good at pushing each other's buttons. As we laugh and watch Dom and Maya dance, I open my mouth to make a comment about the dishwasher never getting started, but I never get to the punchline of the joke.

"Did I walk into a Lovers Quarrel?" Miles asks. He's definitely had one too many of the Mai-Tais, which is shocking, given his refusal of "girly drinks" on every other occasion. He's twirling a small umbrella in his mouth, grinning from ear-to-ear. "Or is it foreplay? How are you two lovebirds? Having a good time?"

"We're good," Livvy says with a laugh. "It's nice to see you." He's so tall that when he leans in to give her a side hug, she doesn't even reach his armpit. It's funny, seeing how petite Livvy is compared to the rest of the guys. She gets along with all of them, and especially now that we're together, it feels more and more like these separate pieces of my life aren't so isolated after all.

"Planning one of these yet?" Miles asks me. "I mean, Liv's way out of your league. You might as well put a ring on it soon, before she finds better."

"Hope you don't mean yourself," I retort playfully. He's right, though. She is out of my league, and oftentimes, I wonder what she's doing with a chump like me. Admittedly though, my grandparents always say the best recipe for marriage is when the other person thinks they got the better end of the bargain. I'd like to think that's true here too.

He places a hand dramatically to his chest. "You wound me. I'm wounded by your cruel words, Alex."

"So sad," I deadpan. I mime playing a tiny violin for

show, and he narrows his eyes at me. If he were a little drunker, I bet he'd even stick out his tongue like this was a grade school argument to be solved with all the old childhood strategies.

"I'm not a relationship man anyway, though. You know that," he adds with a wink.

"You could be one day," Livvy says. "I used to be a man-eater and now I'm an adoptive dog mom of two. Things change."

"Not me," Miles says proudly.

He did, but his past is his own, and it's not job my to dredge it up.

"And how are you, Miles? You found a date yet?" Liv asks.

"Har-har," he remarks. "If you must know, the tall girl over by the DJ set-up has been on my mind all night. I might get her number at the end of the night."

"You mean... Gia?" Liv asks.

"Is that her name? Little weird, but I can work with it."

"Dude, Gia's not really that kind of girl," I say. "She's not dumb enough to fall for your one-night stand lines, and she's my sister's best friend—"

"Hey!" Liv interrupts, indignant.

I amend my statement, "*One of* my sister's best friends. That means you keep your hands and Little Miles to yourself."

"First off, there's nothing *little* about other Miles," he says, "And second, why not let the girl speak for herself?"

Liv and I exchange looks. I usually take her cues about her friends, so when she nods, I shrug. "Suit yourself."

He tosses his mini umbrella into the trash and saunters off, smirking triumphantly on his way to Gia. Admittedly, I'm still getting to know Gia, but I can only assume within minutes of meeting each other, there might be a bloodbath. She seems very progressive and powerful, and he can be a bit of a frat boy. It's a gasoline and blowtorch kind of combination, but I've come to find there are people in this life who learn the hard lessons by being hands-on, and Miles? He's one of those people.

"She's going to eat him alive," Livvy says, clicking her tongue.

I chuckle, sipping my beer. "Abso-fucking-lutely."

I never thought we would find ourselves here. Back when we were two heartbroken kids, I assumed our story ended there, but this second chance at happiness was divine intervention, to say the least. A series of accidents and coincidences and mishaps got us here, but when I look over at Livvy and take in the love of my life, it's worth it, and I'd do it over and over again.

"So are you planning one of these?" she asks. I know she's half-kidding, but the sincerity in her voice immediately catches my attention.

So, I smile. "Of course, but it'll happen much sooner if you catch Maya's bouquet."

She beams. "Deal."

Printed in Great Britain
by Amazon